FIFTY
SHADES *of*
Mr Darcy

FIFTY SHADES *of Mr Darcy*

A PARODY

WILLIAM CODPIECE
THWACKERY

Michael O'Mara Books Limited

First published in Great Britain in 2012 by
Michael O'Mara Books Limited
9 Lion Yard
Tremadoc Road
London SW4 7NQ

A CIP catalogue record for this book is available from the British
Library.

Papers used by Michael O'Mara Books Limited are natural,
recyclable products made from wood grown in sustainable forests.
The manufacturing processes conform to the environmental
regulations of the country of origin.

ISBN: 978-1-84317-996-2 in paperback print format
ISBN: 978-1-84317-997-9 in EPub format
ISBN: 978-1-84317-998-6 in Mobipocket format

Fifty Shades of Mr Darcy is a work of fiction, inspired by other
works of fiction. The appearance and depiction of all characters
in this book, living or dead, fictitious or real, is the result of
the author's own imagination.

1 2 3 4 5 6 7 8 9 10

Printed and bound in Great Britain by
CPI Group (UK) Ltd, Croydon, CR0 4YY

www.mombooks.com

It is a truth universally acknowledged, that a single man in possession of a good riding crop must be in want of a pair of bare buttocks to thrash. At least, that is how it seemed to Elizabeth Bennet. Tied to the bedpost in Mr Darcy's boudoir, her stays unlaced and her bloomers in a state of disarray, trembling in anticipation of the first thwack of leather upon her unblemished skin, she pondered upon the circumstances that had brought her to this most indecorous pass. If Mr Bingley had never come to Netherfield and set his heart upon her sister Jane, then she, Elizabeth, would never have encountered his close friend, Mr Fitzwilliam Darcy. And that one chance meeting was all it had taken for her to be lured into his secret world of hot and horny perverted sex, like a helpless moth drawn towards a candle flame.

Worst of all, she was the mistress of her own undoing. Mr Darcy had made no protestations of love. In fact, he had made his intentions plain from the outset. 'I do not make love, Miss Bennet,' he had told her. 'I bonk. I have it off. I get my end away, I rodger, I boff.'

Could she save this wonderful, sensual man from his own dark desires? Surely if she could but show him how pleasurable genteel nineteenth-century pastimes could be – how a game of backgammon could rival the thrill of nipple clamps, and bonnet-trimming delight the senses as much as the insertion of an XXL butt plug – then he would renounce his S&M ways for good.

But as the first blow fell upon her quivering behind, causing her to cry out in both excitement and pain, that thought was far, far from Elizabeth's mind.

'Oh my!' she gasped. 'What would Lady Catherine say?'

'My dear Mr Bennet,' said Mrs Bennet to her husband, 'have you heard that Netherfield Park is let at last?'

Mr Bennet, his head buried in *A Gentleman's Repository*, merely grunted in reply. Unlike Mrs Bennet's first, second, third and fourth husbands – whom Mrs Bennet had bonked into an early grave – Billy-Bob Bennet was not a man fond of repartee. In short, his sole purpose within the pages of this book is to act as a cipher, to represent an ideal of manliness based on hunting, fishing and DIY, in order to form a striking contrast to the kinky, brooding, slightly prissy anti-hero. Therefore the author couldn't be bothered to give him many words.

'Do you hear me, Mr Bennet?' Mrs Bennet cried impatiently. 'It is to be let to a young man from the north of England, Mr Elliot Bingley, who comes hither in the company of his great friend Mr Fitzwilliam Darcy.'

Mr Bennet sat taciturn, staring at his magazine and waiting for the invention of television.

His wife was in no way discouraged by lack of an audience. 'I have heard,' she continued eagerly, 'that both men are *considerably* well endowed. Both have *huge* packages, I'm told, and now they are come here, to Meryton, with a view, no doubt, to meeting young ladies upon whom they can blow their wads.'

Elizabeth, the second eldest – and arguably hottest – of the Bennet daughters, inwardly winced. Her mother's inappropriate use of street slang and general lack of modesty were often a source of mortification to her and her virtuous elder sister Jane. For instance, why, Elizabeth asked herself, could Mrs Bennet not sit demurely with her hands folded in her lap like any other nineteenth-century matriarch, instead of slumping upon the chaise longue with her legs wide open, so everyone could see her vulgarity?

'Well endowed?' Mary, Mrs Bennet's middle daughter – and arguably the least hot – looked up from her Latin primer and gave her mother a disapproving look. 'It is not seemly to talk thus of gentlemen's fortunes, Mama,' she chided.

'Who said anything about fortunes, girl?' Mrs Bennet replied. 'I am not talking about the size of their *incomes*.' She rolled her eyes in exasperation. Why were her daughters so hopelessly strait-laced? Although her two youngest, Kitty and Lydia, were starting to display signs of interest in the young officers in Town, no doubt she would be in her grave before any of them got laid. Mother to five virgins! It was a torment almost too great to be borne!

'Silly goose,' she scolded Mary. 'A few of their manservants have been talking to the dairymaids in Meryton, and the word is that both gentlemen have simply enormous co ...'

It was a matter of felicity that at the very moment Mrs Bennet was about to utter a word that would have made a courtesan blush, Elizabeth's wayward hair chose to make a dash for a hole in the wainscoting.

'After it, girls!' shrieked Mrs Bennet, as the thick, hugely attractive yet unruly brown mane slithered hither and thither about the floor in a bid to avoid Elizabeth and her sisters, who leapt about, jabbing at it with hairbrushes and ribbons. For a few moments the scene in the drawing room was one of chaos, until Elizabeth – who, like many a romantic heroine, was hopelessly accident-prone – caught her foot on a leg of the card table, and landed upon her lustrous chestnut-tinged curls, wrestling them into a scrunchie.

'There,' she declared, panting, sprawled upon the Aubusson rug, 'I have it under control at last!'

Mrs Bennet looked admiringly at Elizabeth's long, stockinged legs, which had been exposed by her exertions. 'A fine pair!' she thought proudly. 'Just apt for wrapping about the waist of a lieutenant in the Dragoons.' What an irony it was that her daughter was so well shaped for the act of lovemaking, yet displayed precious little interest in the subject. It seemed she would rather be occupied in reading books, wearing hopelessly frumpy clothes and going for bracing walks in the countryside. Mrs Bennet sighed discontentedly. 'Mr Bennet, you will, of course, be paying a visit to Mr Bingley when he comes into the neighbourhood.'

Mr Bennet raised his eyes at last. 'If he shoots, plays pool or has a shed, I shall. If he is one of those newfangled metrosexuals, I shall not.'

'Consider your daughters!' Mrs Bennet continued. 'Jane is twenty-two and Lizzy past twenty, and no one has so much as groped them. If it weren't for Lydia, who I suspect has at least had her fancy tickled by Dick the stablehand, I would lose hope entirely!'

'I do not know why you take on so,' her husband replied. 'Were this the twenty-first century, I agree that it would be preposterous that a twenty-one-year-old, stunningly attractive girl had never so much as held hands with a young man. In fact, I would think it some sort of contrived literary device to make her eventual deflowering all the more salacious. But this is 1813, and it is quite acceptable for a young lady to remain chaste until marriage.'

'Chaste? Chaste? It is easy for *you* to say, Mr Bennet,' exclaimed his wife. '*You* do not have to suffer the neighbourhood talk of "Mrs Bennet's Dykey Daughters"!' Mrs Bennet fanned herself with her copy of *Britain's Hottest Hussars*. 'You will go to see Mr Bingley and Mr Darcy at the earliest opportunity, and ask if either of them fancies a go on one of your daughters. I insist upon it.'

And with that, the matter was settled.

An invitation was soon afterwards dispatched to Netherfield, and Mr Bingley duly visited Mr Bennet and sat with him in his study for ten minutes or so, where an offer of daughter-fondling was formally made. The whole endeavour must have proceeded favourably, as a week later reports reached Longbourn that Mr Bingley was to host a ball, and the Bennet sisters were to be invited. Also to be present were Mr Bingley's two sisters, Looseata and Carrotslime, newly arrived from Town, and his close friend Mr Darcy.

Mrs Bennet could barely contain her excitement. 'I have heard from Lady Lucas that Mr Bingley's balls are legendary!' she exclaimed to anyone who would listen. 'Everyone of quality admires his balls! Until now, sadly, he always held his balls too far away for my daughters to reach. But now he resides at Netherfield his balls are within their grasp!'

At her command, the young Misses Bennet visited Meryton for new trimmings for their best dresses, and long discoursed upon what they would wear. Mrs Bennet had Jane's pale-blue muslin gown adjusted, so that it made her breasts appear the size of ripe pumpkins. Elizabeth, however, resisted her mother's entreaties to don a leather minidress and white ankle boots and settled instead for a dress of plain cream calico. Cragg, the housekeeper – having strong, although unpleasantly gnarled, working-class hands – managed to knot her unruly hair into a simple braid.

Glancing in the looking glass, Elizabeth sighed. With her alabaster skin and full lips, she thought herself not so pretty as Jane, whose strawberry-blonde locks attracted so much attention. She would never draw admiring glances, she decided, with so many faults; her breasts were too pert, her legs too long and shapely, and her vivid blue eyes too large and limpid. And what man would want her once he knew about her magical vibrating vagina? No, matters of the heart were not for her.

Elizabeth's needless worries were dispelled at once, however, by the merry nature of the gathering at Netherfield. Mr Bingley himself was the most genial of hosts – a gentleman with an easy, cheerful manner, a pleasing countenance and blue eyes that shone in mirth. He lost no time in exhorting every lady in the assembly to dance. He launched himself into the Gay Gordons with aplomb, could not seem to have enough of Lord Percy's Yardstick, and cried out in delight at The Captain's Hornpipe. Elizabeth could see at once that Mr Bingley had made a favourable impression upon Jane; her sister remarked at length upon his muscular body, his cherubic blond curls and the cut of his jib. His jib, in fact, escaped no one's notice – it was enormous.

'Truly, he is a most affable character,' she remarked. 'I fancy, though, that he is not the most intelligent of men.'

'Whatever makes you think that?' Elizabeth replied.

'Oh, it is but a supposition. Based on the fact that when I asked him how he was enjoying our shire, he replied that Arseshire was the prettiest of counties, but he had been mistakenly pronouncing it "Hertfordshire".'

'Intelligence matters little, if his general nature is as agreeable as you say,' Elizabeth replied, watching Mr Bingley punching himself in the face over the punchbowl. Her attention was soon diverted, however, to Bingley's friend Mr Darcy, who stood in the corner of the room with his back to the company, busily arranging some dusty tomes on the bookshelf into alphabetical order. 'How inconsiderate,' thought Elizabeth, 'not to dance when there are so many young ladies left without a partner.' She could not help noting, however, Mr Darcy's athletic physique. He must have stood six feet two or three inches in his Cuban-heeled riding boots; his carriage was upright, his shoulders broad and his buttocks firm and well sculpted. Elizabeth felt a pull in some dark, secret place inside her belly. It might have been her spleen. Or then again, perhaps it was her G-spot. Having received minimal schooling and being largely ignorant of female anatomy, she could not be entirely certain. Just as she was musing on her inner organs, Mr Bingley called out to his friend.

'Hullo there, Darcy! Do come and dance!'

Mr Darcy turned and – *oh my!* – Elizabeth saw his face for the first time. His lips were sensual and full, his ginger hair – no, wait a minute, let's call it copper – hung down over grey eyes so alluring they could have been hammered from boulders of solid sex. *He was so freakin' hot!*

'There are ladies waiting,' Bingley implored him. 'Leave the books and come hither.'

Darcy's sculpted lips curled up into a disdainful smile.

'Normally I would dance,' said he. 'And expertly – just as I do all other things. However, I must *whip* this bookshelf into shape. Some fool has put Lord Byron before William Blake, do you see?'

'Oh, that will have been me!' cried Bingley happily. 'You know how hoples i am at speling! But come, Darcy, I beg you to desist! Why concern yourself with books when you can dance with some delightful young ladies? There are many lovely creatures here tonight. What about that pretty young thing over there with the humungous chest?'

Darcy's lips quirked up into a sneer. 'You mean Miss Shapen? She is not to my taste.'

'What of Miss Anthrope?'

'Too miserable.'

'Miss Laid?'

'She sounds promising. Where is she?'

'I just lost sight of her.'

Darcy gave an exasperated sigh. 'None here can tempt me. You, my friend, have been dancing with the only true beauty here tonight.'

Mr Bingley beamed with happiness. 'Jane Bennet? She is most agreeable, is she not? But what about her sister, Elizabeth? Is she not a handsome creature also?'

'Hmmm …' Darcy appeared lost in thought. 'She is tolerable, I suppose,' he said eventually. 'But too innocent-looking to tempt me. And her mother is a vulgar creature.' He turned his steely gaze in the direction of Mrs Bennet, who was dirty-dancing with a young fusilier. 'Look at her tattoos. What is that large one upon her shoulder? Is it a penis?'

Mr Bingley peered. 'I'm not sure, I think it may be some sort of jellyfish.'

'In any case, it is badly done.'

Elizabeth, who had overheard every word of their exchange, lost no time in telling her acquaintants with much wit and playfulness how she had been spurned by

Mr Bingley's proud and disdainful friend. But privately, her spirits were much affronted. There was no denying that she thought Mr Darcy the most handsome billionaire she had ever seen. Gazing upon his lithe frame propping up the bookshelf, one leg cocked at a rakish angle, the other leg arranged at a cockish angle, she felt a jolt of energy coursing through her body. Elizabeth wondered what it would be like to take a turn about the rose garden in the company of such a man. Or to sit in the shade of an arbour, reading Wordsworth together. At the very thought of a mutual poetry-reading session, her body gave another little shiver of excitement.

'I think he's dangerous,' her Subconscious counselled. 'Keep well away from him.'

'God, you're so frigid,' her Inner Slapper interjected.

'Does anyone else think he might be gay?' her Gaydar piped up. 'I mean, check out the paisley cravat.'

While her inner voices sparred, and Elizabeth berated herself for forgetting her medication, Mrs Bennet came whirling across the room accompanied by four young officers of the militia. Evidently, she had partaken liberally of the rum punch, and her face glowed like a beacon.

'These nice young gentlemen have offered to take me outside and show me their manoeuvres!' she exclaimed. 'Captain Yates here tells me his musket is half-cocked already, and with my help it will be fully cocked in no time.'

Elizabeth noticed that Mr Darcy had turned his attention to their party, and was staring at her with those unsettling, penetrating grey eyes of his. She turned crimson with shame. Her mother's lack of decorum would once again be the talk of Meryton, no doubt.

'I will join you boys in just a moment, but I must find a chamber pot first!' Mrs Bennet exclaimed. 'I swear I have already piddled in my pantaloons!' Her gaze landed upon

Mr Darcy. 'Lor, that must be the Mr Darcy I have heard so much about! Well, I can see that what they say is true – he is *so freakin' hot*! Is he not hot, Lizzy?'

Elizabeth placed her finger upon her lips, in an attempt to signal to her mother that their conversation might be overheard.

'I imagine if Mr Darcy is overly warm, he will see it upon himself to step away from the fireplace,' she whispered.

'I was not referring to his temperature, child. I am speaking of his appearance,' Mrs Bennet trilled, fanning herself with what Elizabeth realized, with horror, was a pair of bloomers.

'His breeches are snug-fitting after the London fashion, do you not notice, Lizzy? In fact, when he stands there in the firelight you can clearly see the outline of his –'

'Shuttlecock?' Bingley interjected. 'We are setting up the card tables in the drawing room if you care to make up a party.' He looked from Elizabeth's scarlet countenance to Mr Darcy's dark, glowering one. 'Or we can play whist, if you prefer?'

With one last penetrating look at Elizabeth, Fitzwilliam Darcy turned on his Cuban heels and stalked off towards the gaming tables. Elizabeth, mortified and exasperated all at once, turned her attention back to the dancers, determined to put all thought of Mr Bingley's arrogant friend out of her head.

Yet, that night, she dreamt of loosening her stays under his steely grey gaze, as if in a daze. While lost in a maze, with her bloomers ablaze.

It had been one of those days.

When Elizabeth and Jane were alone in Jane's bedchamber

the next morning, the latter expressed to her sister how very much she admired Mr Bingley.

'Oh, Lizzy, although we are not well acquainted, I cannot help but feel a great deal of affection for him already. So what if he is a trifle dim-witted? He is also handsome, agreeable and good humoured.'

'He is all of those things, indeed,' Elizabeth replied. 'And, I believe, he admires you, too.'

'I cannot allow myself to think so. After all, he danced with me but twice.' Jane tossed her strawberry-blonde locks. Elizabeth caught them deftly and threw them back. 'But he did try to touch me up on the balcony.'

'There! That proves it! He returns your affections!'

'Dear Lizzy, do you think it can be true?'

'It was plain to all! But sweet sister, be wary. You have met him but once, and his reputation ...'

'There are rumours of impropriety?'

'Oh, Jane ...' Elizabeth sighed. 'Carrotslime Bingley told me that in Town, among the ladies of fashion, he is known as "Mr Bang-Me". But we only have her word for that. I, for one, am convinced there is little truth in the matter.'

'And what of you, dear sister? Slighted by Mr Fitzwilliam Darcy! Are you affronted?'

'Indeed, I am not,' Elizabeth smiled. 'If Mr Darcy considers himself above our station, I can understand it. After all, our stepfather has but two thousand pounds a year, and Mr Darcy is a man of vast wealth, and well known for his charitable works.'

'Indeed, his educational foundation is spoken of highly,' agreed Jane. 'Its aim, I believe, is to introduce corporal punishment into every finishing school for young ladies. There is much to admire in his philanthropy.'

'If not his character,' added Elizabeth. Although, inside her head, her Subconscious and her Inner Slapper were having a bitch-fight in a metaphorical car park.

'Admit it – there is something about Mr Darcy that attracts you!' shouted her Inner Slapper, grabbing a handful of her Subconscious's hair.

'Oww! Don't listen to her!' her Subconscious yelled, forcing her Inner Slapper into a headlock. 'He's dangerous. And anally retentive. Did you notice the way he rearranged the ornaments on the mantelpiece? He did it with a tape measure, for Christ's sake!'

Elizabeth shook her head, forcing herself out of her reverie.

'Do not worry,' she reassured Jane, whose lovely face radiated sisterly concern. 'I shall soon forget Mr Darcy's insult. I will endeavour to put him behind me.'

Jane gave a wry smile. 'Behind you? I fear that is exactly where he would be if Mama has her way.'

Following Mr Bingley's ball, the ladies of Longbourn fast became better acquainted with those of Netherfield. Miss Jane Bennet's pleasing manners grew on the goodwill of Mr Bingley's sisters, and she was oft invited to spend time in their company.

Looseata and Carrotslime made a great pet of Jane, and together the young ladies passed many an afternoon decrying other people's dress sense, and waiting for someone to ask them to marry them. On occasion they would be diverted by some small project, such as knitting balaclavas for the terminally ugly of the parish, and one such scheme led to a letter being delivered to Longbourn early one morning.

My dear friend Jane,
We do entreat you to dine with Looseata and me today. We are planning to submit a little piece to *The Lady's Fancy Bits* about the philanthropic works of our mutual friend Mr Darcy, and given your eloquence and skill at letter-writing, we are quite determined that you should be the author of the same. Come and discuss the matter as soon as you can on receipt of this.

Yours ever, Carrotslime Bingley

'May I take the carriage?' asked Jane.

'Certainly not,' replied Mrs Bennet. 'You must go on horseback, because it seems likely to rain and then you must stay all night. And you can pretend to be saddle-sore, and ask Mr Bingley to rub your inner thighs.'

Thus the matter was decided, and Jane set off on horseback the three miles to Netherfield. Before long her mother's prayers were answered, and it began to rain hard. Elizabeth was deeply concerned for her sister, but Mrs Bennet was delighted with the turn of events.

'When she arrives at Netherfield her dress will be quite soaked through!' she declared. 'Do you not think so, Mr Bennet?'

Mr Bennet, who was a poorly developed character in every way, merely shrugged.

'Her nipples will be poking through the muslin like chapel hat pegs! Mr Bingley cannot fail to take notice!'

And indeed, the very next morning a note arrived from Netherfield, addressed to Elizabeth.

My dearest sister,
I find myself very unwell this morning, which, I suppose, is to be imputed to my getting wet through

yesterday. Mr Bingley says I have a congestion of the chest, which he is seeking to ease by assiduous hourly massages. He says he fears I will have to stay abed until he has quite rubbed the affliction out of me. All of this means I will be unable to write my character study of Fitzwilliam Darcy for *The Lady's Fancy Bits*, as I so faithfully promised Carrotslime Bingley. Would you be so gracious as to take my place, Lizzy? Please say yes.

Yours, Jane

Elizabeth was conflicted. While her compassionate heart urged her to be with her sister at this most worrying time, she was anxious to keep her distance from Mr Darcy. After much cogitation and anxious pacing of the parlour, at length she made her decision.

'Mother, I must go to Jane. Bingley's ministrations are well intentioned, no doubt, but I cannot believe they will result in much easing of her symptoms.'

Mrs Bennet was exasperated. 'She is being well taken care of, Lizzy! It is but a trifling cold! And Mr Bingley is unlikely to get past first base if Jane is to be chaperoned by *you*.'

Nevertheless, Elizabeth insisted, and when no horse could be found to accommodate her, she determined to walk the short distance to Netherfield across the fields. She leapt over stiles, sprang over puddles and – being hopelessly accident-prone in a cute yet vulnerable way that made all red-blooded men want to shag her – she arrived thither with her dress in shreds and her ankle shattered in several places, and was shown into the breakfast parlour.

The Misses Bingley were aghast at her appearance, and shrieked aloud at the muddy state of her petticoats.

'And what, pray, has happened to your hair?' asked

Carrotslime Bingley, as tendrils of Elizabeth's mane escaped from under her bonnet and tried to head towards the French windows.

But Mr Darcy stared upon her countenance with such intent that her cheeks turned even ruddier than before.

'It is thrilling to see a young lady so invigorated by exercise,' he murmured, never taking his slate-grey eyes off her own. 'I am a great believer in it as a *discipline*.'

Elizabeth's enquiries after Jane's health were politely answered, and after breakfast she was able to visit her in her bedchamber. Mr Bingley leapt up from the bedside as soon as she entered.

'Why Miss Bennet!' he exclaimed. 'I was just about to deliver your sister's daily treatment!'

It was evident that in his anxiety for her sister's health, Mr Bingley had barely rested – his attire betrayed him. His breeches were loosed, and his shirt was unlaced, and his face bore the look of someone who had spent the night tossing, and possibly turning, too.

Elizabeth crossed to Jane's bedside. Her sister was flush of face and breathing heavily.

'Jane, my dearest, I am here now. I shall nurse you until you are well. Mr Bingley, pray summon the apothecary.'

'I will send someone at once,' he replied, tucking his shirt hastily into his breeches. 'I'll be back soon, Snuggle Bunny.'

Jane smiled weakly. 'Don't be long, Dumpling.'

When Bingley had quit the room, Elizabeth turned down Jane's bedsheets. Thankfully, they dealt with rejection pretty well – they were turned down every day.

'I'm so grateful to see you, Lizzy,' Jane murmured. 'Yet I am loath to ask you to take on my duties as scribe, as well as those of nursemaid. *The Lady's Fancy Bits* will have to do without an article about Fitzwilliam Darcy.'

'Hush, now, do not tire yourself,' chided Elizabeth, gently. 'I will take on your journalistic duties gladly. I am a great reader of novels, as you know. Indeed, on the strength of that alone, I would no doubt be able to breeze into a job in a prestigious publishing house *just like that*, should such opportunities for young ladies ever exist in the future.'

'So you will speak with Mr Darcy, even though you abhor him so?'

'For you, Jane, I would do much more,' replied Elizabeth tenderly.

'It is agreed then.' Jane settled back gratefully onto her pillow, and soon her breathing settled into the steady rhythm of sleep. Elizabeth kept watch upon the invalid, occasionally mopping Jane's brow and at other times dusting and polishing it, but after a while took down a book of poems from the bookshelf and began to read.

Meanwhile, downstairs in the breakfast room, the talk was of the second eldest Miss Bennet, and the exhibition she had made of herself. Her manners were dissected and pronounced to be very ill indeed, a mixture of pride and impertinence. In short, she had no style, no taste, no beauty.

'My, did you note her countenance on her arrival?' remarked Looseata Bingley. 'She looked entirely wild!'

'To walk three miles! What abominable independence!' declared her sister.

'And what of her petticoat? Six inches deep in mud!'

'All was lost upon me,' Bingley said gallantly. 'I confess I did not notice her petticoat. Did you, Darcy?'

'Indeed not,' replied Mr Darcy. 'I was far too busy looking at her tits.'

When luncheon was over and the rest of the party were at the card table, Elizabeth petitioned Mr Darcy for an hour of his time, that she might discern from him some facts that might pique the interest of readers of *The Lady's Fancy Bits*.

'You flatter me, Miss Bennet, to suggest that young ladies may have any curiosity about my life and day-to-day business,' Darcy remarked. 'I hardly think myself a fit subject for anyone to study. Moreover, speaking about myself gives me little pleasure.'

'Rest assured, Mr Darcy, it will afford me little pleasure either,' Elizabeth replied archly. 'I think we are both of an understanding in that regard.'

Nonetheless, together they repaired to the drawing room, where Elizabeth laid out her notebook and writing pencils upon an occasional table, which was keen to let people know that it was only occasionally a table – most of the time it was a wingback chair. While she did so, she could not help observing that Mr Darcy's eyes were fixed upon her.

'If you think to embarrass me, Sir, with your scrutiny, be informed that I am not intimidated easily,' she said airily. 'If there is something about my behaviour or appearance that you find reprehensible, pray tell me, that I might seek to rectify it at once.'

Mr Darcy smiled.

Oh my! His mouth was so ... so ... *mouthish!*

'I make no such observation, Miss Bennet,' he replied. 'I was merely wondering how it would be to take up one of those fine pencils of yours, and to insert it, oh so slowly ...'

Elizabeth's heart thudded in her chest.

' ... into a pencil sharpener,' he continued, his grey eyes dancing wickedly, like two evil imps high on cider.

At that moment, a servant Elizabeth did not recognize,

his hair cropped close and his visage roughly stubbled, appeared from behind a potted-plant stand.

'Ah, Taylor,' said Mr Darcy. 'Have you made your final appraisal as regards Miss Bennet?'

'I have, Sir,' replied Taylor.

'And your conclusion?'

'34C, Sir.'

'Good! Then make haste to Meryton.'

Taylor gave a curt bow, and headed for the door.

'My manservant, Taylor, has been despatched to buy some new undergarments for you,' Darcy remarked, by way of explanation. 'I could not help noticing that your bloomers and stays were sullied during your journey from Longbourn.'

Elizabeth bristled. Mr Darcy's impertinence seemingly knew no bounds!

'I assure you, I have no need of charity, Sir,' Elizabeth replied, both abashed and affronted. 'My underthings may not be as finely stitched, nor as decoratively embroidered, as those belonging to the Misses Bingley, but they are perfectly adequate for my needs.'

'And what exactly are your *needs*, Miss Bennet?' Mr Darcy asked playfully.

'I have no *needs*, as you put it, Sir.'

'You just said you did.'

God, he was an arse. 'I think you understand my meaning perfectly, Mr Darcy,' Elizabeth said firmly. 'And please, no gifts.'

Mr Darcy looked disappointed. 'Please indulge me, Miss Bennet,' he said in a low voice, edging a little closer towards her on the chaise longue. 'I am an inordinately wealthy man, and if I wish to buy you a silk shift with little cut-out bits that allow just a fleeting glimpse of nipple, that is my prerogative. Or satin bloomers that cling, like water, to your firm young ...'

Mr Darcy's eyes were now taking on a feverish intensity. Elizabeth decided it was in everyone's best interests to cut him short.

'Pray, do not embarrass me again, Sir. I cannot accept your gifts. I have no wish to be beholden to you.'

'You are refusing me?' Mr Darcy looked puzzled. He cocked his head to one side. Then cocked it to the other side. Then cocked his leg for good measure.

'You are fond of cocking, Sir?' Elizabeth enquired.

'Oh, I am, Miss Bennet,' Mr Darcy murmured. '*Very* fond indeed.'

'Come now, let's move the plot along!' shouted Elizabeth's Subconscious.

Glancing down at her notebook, Elizabeth read the first of her questions in as commanding a voice as she could muster. 'You have vast wealth at your disposal. Pray tell, how is it possible to manage your estates and business interests so successfully?'

'By exercising the *strictest* control,' Mr Darcy replied. 'I have over four hundred servants at Pemberley, and those who do not meet my exacting standards, or who displease me, are soon beaten into shape.'

'You are speaking metaphorically, I trust?'

'No. I personally pull down their breeches and give them twenty strokes. Next question, Miss Bennet.'

'Pemberley is considered one of the foremost houses in the county of Derbyshire, if not in all of England. What do you consider to be its finest merits?'

Mr Darcy gave a wicked smile. 'Firstly, you must inform the young ladies who read your magazine that I am changing the name of my estate.'

'Indeed, Mr Darcy?'

'To *Memberley*.'

Elizabeth fought to keep her composure. She would not be baited into responding to his puerile schoolboy humour.

'You must do me the honour of visiting, Miss Bennet,' Mr Darcy continued. 'There is much there that I would like to show you. I have decorated many rooms after the French fashion. You would pass many a happy hour there, I'm sure, fingering my *bibelots*.'

Elizabeth, occupied by the hurried writing of notes, was grateful to be looking down at her notebook so Mr Darcy could not see the blush that was now starting to spread across her cheeks.

'Aside from calling upon friends in the country, how do you spend your time?'

'I sail. I indulge in various physical pursuits. I ride – hard. And I get up whenever I can in Charlie Tango.'

'Charlie Tango? Is that your hot-air balloon?'

'No, he's my rent boy.'

'*I knew it!*' yelled her Gaydar.

Seeing her discomfiture, Mr Darcy appeared to soften. 'I am toying with you, Miss Bennet,' he said in an amused voice. 'Yes, Charlie Tango is my hot-air balloon.'

'And your charitable pursuits? Are they close to your heart?'

Mr Darcy's smile instantly vanished. 'Some would say I have no heart, Miss Bennet.'

'How can that be so, Mr Darcy?'

'There is, I believe, in every disposition a tendency to some particular evil, a natural defect, which not even the best education can overcome.'

He leant closer, and Elizabeth could smell his enticing, manly smell – she sensed cologne, linen, leather and something else. Pickled onions, perhaps?

'I have many vices,' Mr Darcy said huskily. 'My libido,

for one, I dare not vouch for. It is, I believe, too little yielding.'

'That is a failing indeed!' cried Elizabeth. 'Implacable lust is a shade in a character.'

'I have many shades, Miss Bennet,' said Mr Darcy. 'About fifty, last time I counted.'

The invalid being not much improved, and dusk drawing on, Elizabeth was invited to stay overnight at Netherfield. She passed a great deal of it in Jane's room, but was much disturbed by Mr Bingley knocking upon the door several times during the night, obviously desirous of administering to her sister himself. Carrotslime and Looseata also called in upon them before they made their way to bed, keen to enquire after Jane's health and to be a pair of complete bitches.

'Mr Darcy informed us that you have "very fine eyes",' the elder Miss Bingley remarked. 'If you were not of such low social status and diminished means, I would declare him to be in love with you!'

'I cannot imagine Mr Darcy has any tender feelings,' Elizabeth replied coolly. 'He seems to be a man of large appetite and little delicacy, and unused to female company.'

'It is true that he shuns the company of our sex,' complained Looseata. 'When he is in Town, he is most often to be found at his Club, Spanky's.'

'A shame indeed,' added Carrotslime, 'that a gentleman of his fortune and position should be a confirmed bachelor. Still, when he marries – as all men must – he will doubtless choose someone of his own standing in society. Like myself, perhaps.'

'It would be a good match,' Elizabeth declared, with

much sincerity, for at this time she could imagine no better spouse for Mr Darcy than this vain and prattling creature.

'And what of your own matrimonial hopes, Miss Elizabeth Bennet?' Carrotslime continued. 'Perhaps some impoverished clergyman might take a fancy to you, or, if you are exceedingly fortunate, a farmer?'

'Cow!' hissed Elizabeth's Subconscious. 'I harbour no such hopes. I am content with my reading, and my country walks. Love holds little attraction for me.'

'Indeed. No doubt that is why you pay so little attention to fashion. Your lack of interest in the opposite sex would explain your hopelessly outmoded clothes.'

Elizabeth bristled again – she really should shave her legs. 'I am fortunate enough to have a benefactor in that regard,' she remarked. 'Mr Darcy has sent to Town for new undergarments for me. In the finest silk and satin.'

Carrotslime Bingley seemed taken aback. 'Mr Darcy? Buying gifts for you?' Then she seemed to recover herself. 'How like him to be generous! He has taken pity on your family, no doubt, and your greatly reduced circumstances. He is an ample benefactor of the poor and needy.'

With that she took her leave, and with Looseata following close behind, the two Bennet sisters were presently left alone.

'How kind-hearted Carrotslime and Looseata are,' Jane remarked. 'They are *such* good friends to us.'

Elizabeth could only sigh. Jane was such a dumb-ass sometimes.

The following morning, Jane's health was much improved, and Elizabeth wrote immediately to her mother, to beg that the carriage might be sent for them during the course of the day. Mrs Bennet's reply, however, dashed all her hopes of an imminent return to Longbourn.

> *My dear girls,*
> Have either of you managed to ensnare any of the young gentlemen yet? I am loath to send for you until you have. Jane, you must hitch up the hem of your gown a little; no, make that a *lot*. You have such shapely thighs, you must show them off to Mr Bingley. And Elizabeth, pray, do not *read books* in front of the gentlemen, lest they think you a lesbian. You will have more chance of securing the gentlemen's attention if you giggle girlishly at their witticisms, and, when they win at cards, shriek with excitement while jumping up and down so your bubbies wobble like jellies. It has always worked for me.
> Your loving Mother

Elizabeth, who had little intention of giggling or shrieking, and was determined at all costs to avoid wobbling, urged Jane to borrow Mr Bingley's carriage, and at length it was settled that their original design of leaving Netherfield that morning should be carried out.

This communication excited many professions of concern, and they were pressed to stay on at least another day. Mr Bingley, in particular, seemed keen to continue administering to Jane, declaring that his regular massages were having many beneficial effects. To Elizabeth, however, their departure was a welcome relief. Close proximity to Mr Darcy over the past day had produced in her a tumult of emotions, chief among them vexation that she could be so powerfully physically attracted to someone who was so evidently a twat.

After taking tea in the parlour, the sisters took their leave. Carrotslime Bingley proclaimed herself distraught over Jane's departure, and the young ladies parted with promises to meet very soon. To Elizabeth, who was mounting the steps of the carriage, she remarked, 'Oh! You have something all over your face, Lizzy.'

Elizabeth reached up a hand to brush her cheek. 'Is it cake crumbs?' she enquired.

'No,' Carrotslime declared in a voice too low for anyone else to hear. 'It's *poverty*.'

Mr Darcy stood erect on the steps of Netherfield, his gaze fixed upon Elizabeth, running one of his long index fingers back and forth across his upper lip.

Is that just some sort of tic, like the lip quirking and head cocking, or is he trying to tell me something? Elizabeth wondered, searching in her valise for her pocket mirror to see whether her moustache needed bleaching. Under his scrutiny, she sensed a blush creep up her cheeks. She could feel his grey eyes burning into her, like red-hot pokers stirring the coals of her desire. The more they poked, the higher her flames of longing rose, until the metaphor exploded in a burst of sparks and badly written prose.

Yet if Elizabeth had hopes to forget Mr Fitzwilliam Darcy and his poking eyes, it was not to be. A week after she and Jane had returned from Netherfield, the Bennets were invited to attend a gathering at the home of Sir William Lucas and his unfortunate-looking daughter Charlotte. With a face like a King Edward potato and a figure to match, Charlotte was deemed unlikely to catch the eye of any suitor, and destined, seemingly, to remain an old maid. Yet what she lacked in good looks, she more than made up for in liveliness of spirit.

'I do declare, this party totally sucks,' Charlotte complained to Elizabeth and Jane as they took a turn about the parlour together. 'Father can be such a lame-ass. I don't suppose either of you have any drugs?'

Both sisters shook their heads in bewilderment.

'Then at least we should have some music,' said Charlotte determinedly, beckoning Elizabeth towards the pianoforte. 'Come, Elizabeth, let us have "Willy Is Everything To Me".'

Elizabeth demurred. 'My talents upon the pianoforte are meagre, as you know,' she said modestly. 'I would rather not sit down before those who must be in the habit of hearing only the very best performers.'

'Oh, but Elizabeth, if you do not play, I shall have to start self-harming,' entreated Charlotte.

With great reluctance, Elizabeth arranged herself upon the piano stool, and fingered the keys gingerly.

'I did not know that you liked to *play*, Miss Bennet.'

Holy stalker! Where did he come from? Looming over the pianoforte, his flint-grey eyes boring into hers as though trying to tunnel right through her eye sockets, down her neck and through her stomach and intestines to her vagina, was none other than Mr Fitzwilliam Darcy.

'I like to *play*, too.' His tongue caressed the words. Elizabeth was suddenly thankful she was sitting on the piano stool, as her legs seemed to have turned to water.

'Would you care to play together, Miss Bennet?' Mr Darcy stroked his bottom lip with a long index finger. Jeez, it was long – it must have been nearly ten inches. Her huge blue eyes widened to the size of saucers.

'D'you think he's huge all over?' her Inner Slapper asked slyly. 'Go on, take a look at his feet. You know what they say ...'

Elizabeth glanced down. How could she not have noticed it before? Fitzwilliam Darcy's feet were the largest and the thickest in girth of any she'd seen in her life. She swallowed nervously.

'It was my intention to play "Good Morning, Pretty Maid." Are you familiar with the lyrics, Mr Darcy?'

Mr Darcy's lips quirked up into a smile. 'Oh, I am *bound* by many things, Miss Bennet, but never by convention,' he murmured. 'I shall sing my own lyrics. Begin!'

With trembling fingers, Elizabeth began to sound out the first notes of the familiar air.

'Good morning, pretty maid,
Whither are you heading?'

Mr Darcy's voice was disconcertingly low and sensual. He had moved behind her now, to the back of the piano stool, and she could feel his hot breath caressing her neck.

'To Gloucester, if it please you
For 'tis my sister's wedding.'

'Fair maid, it does not please me
It gives me much vexation
I told you to stay home
And eat a pound of bacon.'

'Good sir, please stay your hand
It's true I have not eaten.'
'A wicked miss you've been
And now you must be beaten!'

Thwack, whack, smack!
Three strokes he did deliver

Thwack, whack, smack!
Her flesh was all a-quiver.

'If you disobey me
You're sure to be berated
I'll flog you with my riding crop
Until I'm fully sated!'
Thwack, whack ...'

It was at this point in the proceedings that Elizabeth felt her body begin to sway.

'Take care, Sir, she faints!' shouted Sir William.

In an instant, Mr Darcy had swooped down and gripped Elizabeth's slender frame tightly in his attractive arms.

'Fetch some smelling salts!' Charlotte called out.

'Forget the smelling salts,' Mr Darcy growled, his eyes, blazing with concern, locked on to Elizabeth's. 'What this young lady needs is sausages – lots of them. And maybe some eggs and pancakes with maple syrup on the side.'

The servants at once rushed hither and thither and Mr Darcy, hooking his freakishly long index fingers under Elizabeth's armpits – *holy sweat glands, why hadn't someone invented deodorant yet!* – lifted her gently onto a nearby chaise longue.

'Let us give Miss Bennet time to recover,' he commanded, waving away the crowds of anxious friends and acquaintances, and the hordes of officers who had gathered in the hope of catching a glimpse of her knickers.

'You gave us quite a scare, Miss Bennet,' he whispered, brushing a tendril of her hair gently behind her ear.

'Oh my! I have no idea what came over me,' Elizabeth murmured. Mr Darcy was gazing at her so intently, she found it impossible to meet his eye.

'If I had known my song would shock you so, I would

not have performed it,' continued Mr Darcy, tucking another tendril of hair behind her other ear.

'No, Sir, please do not think your song offended me. It was a most ... unusual ditty.'

'Oh, it was just a little something I wrote when I was but a boy at Beaton.'

'You attended Beaton?' asked Elizabeth, wide-eyed. But of course! Now it all became clear why Mr Darcy was the way he was. In the English Public Schools Annual League Table, Beaton came top every year in Flogging, Fagging, Ruggering *and* Buggering. That kind of education had to have an effect upon a child. Suddenly she could picture Fitzwilliam Darcy as a young, innocent boy, being forced to listen to endless dirty jokes and to fag for the senior boys, trying not to cry as the housemaster thwacked him again and again with his yardstick ...

'Indeed. My parents would have engaged a tutor, but my mother's friend, Lady Catherine de Burgh, who had great influence over her, insisted upon my attending.' Mr Darcy looped both tendrils of Lizzy's hair together at the back of her head, worked them into a French plait, and sat back to admire his handiwork.

'You are a beguiling woman, Miss Bennet,' he murmured. 'I find you most intriguing.'

Elizabeth blushed to the roots of her now beautifully coiffed hair. 'Um, *hello*?' her Gaydar interjected. 'Is no one else thinking what *I'm* thinking?'

But Elizabeth paid no heed. This man, this beautiful, sensual man, was intrigued by her! And she feared that she was, against all wise judgement, becoming equally drawn to him.

'I do believe you would not have fainted if you had eaten before you came here, Miss Bennet,' Mr Darcy continued. 'A young lady should take nourishment at least five times a day.'

'I rarely feel hungry, Mr Darcy. But thank you for your concern.'

Mr Darcy's eyes darkened.

'You must eat more, Miss Bennet! I insist upon it!'

At once, Elizabeth's mood changed from one of desire to one of annoyance. 'You *insist*? You presume too much, Mr Darcy. We are of but meagre acquaintance. Insistence is the preserve of those with whom I enjoy more intimate friendship.'

Mr Darcy's eyes were blazing now, like a malfunctioning boiler. 'I do not like to be defied, Miss Bennet,' he breathed huskily. 'If indeed I knew you more intimately, I should put you across my knee and spank you!'

Spank her? Now Elizabeth felt light-headed again. 'I would remind you, Sir, that we are in polite company. And talk of spanking is both indecorous and insulting.' Now her own blue eyes blazed, too, with humiliation and anger.

Mr Darcy stared at her for a long moment. His brow creased, and his expression was pained, as if he was torn between two choices – a cheese sandwich vs tuna mayo, maybe, or between pride and desire.

All of a sudden, he stood and gave a curt bow.

'Laters, Baby,' he said stiffly, and turned upon his heel.

'Seriously, what a knobend,' muttered her Subconscious.

But that night Elizabeth dreamt of intense grey eyes, muscly arms and huge, throbbing feet.

The village of Longbourn was only one mile from Meryton, a most convenient distance for the young Bennet ladies, who were tempted thither three or four times a week to visit the milliner's or to run various errands for their mother and stepfather. Lydia and Kitty were ever more frequent visitors now that a whole regiment of the militia had settled in the neighbourhood for the winter, and even Mrs Bennet was fond of accompanying the girls there for the opportunity of casting her eye upon a pleasing male form made ever more appealing by close-fitting army breeches.

It happened that Elizabeth walked with her two younger sisters to the village one morning, despite a light autumn drizzle, in order that she might visit the haberdashers for buttons and patronize the poor of the parish with a basket of groceries. Before long, Kitty and Lydia had become distracted by the sight of a red jacket.

'Why, there is Captain Carter!' Lydia declared. 'Look, Kitty, he is just coming out of Slaggy Sal's hovel – I do wonder why he has been visiting *her*. Pray, let us waylay him and ask!'

Thus the sisters parted company and Elizabeth continued her walk alone, crossing the village green at a quick pace and tripping over, vulnerably yet somehow sexily, upon the steps of the haberdashery shop.

'Allow me, Miss Bennet.'

Oh, this was insufferable! Here, yet again, was Fitzwilliam Darcy, the last person she hoped to see in Meryton. His hair was tousled from the rain, and his grey eyes sparkled silver in the dull morning light. He was holding out his powerful hand in order to help her up. Reluctantly, Elizabeth allowed him to lift her from the step, and, using a pocket handkerchief he had taken from his waistcoat, delicately remove one of her teeth from where it had become embedded in her lower lip.

'I worry for your safety, Miss Bennet,' he murmured, gently dabbing the blood from her chin. 'It is clearly not healthy for you to be walking about on your own. I will see to it that Taylor accompanies you in future.'

'Good morning, Miss Bennet.' Taylor's head suddenly poked out from behind a horse trough beside the shop. *Jeez, he got everywhere!*

Elizabeth would have demurred – she was perfectly able to perambulate the neighbourhood unaccompanied – but her mouth still smarted and, under Mr Darcy's penetrating stare, she somehow found herself unable to argue.

'Now, Miss Bennet, we must get you out of this rain.' His eyes surveyed her gown and petticoat. 'You are wet, I see.' Now they ran over her embonpoint. 'And I am stiff ...'

Elizabeth felt a blush blooming from her cheeks down to her chest.

'Stiff, Mr Darcy?'

'Indeed. Bingley and I engaged in an archery contest yesterday. And I fear my aching arms cannot hold this door open for long. Come ...'

She knew not why, but she felt powerless to resist his entreaty. Stepping inside the shop, she feigned concentration, shaking the raindrops from her gown as she tried to regain her composure. *Holy catalogue model!* Mr Darcy was the very picture of early nineteenth-century hotness. His white linen shirt was freshly pressed and open at the collar, while his grey flannel trousers hung off his hips in a most distracting fashion.

'What brings you to Meryton, Miss Bennet?'

Mr Darcy's sensuous, low voice startled her from her reverie.

'Necessity, Mr Darcy. I have a basket of eggs for Granny Egbert, and some butter for Sergeant Butterworth. Oh, and Mr Sexpest requested I bring him some of my unwashed underthings.'

'You are visiting the needy?' Mr Darcy looked pleasantly surprised. 'It is most commendable for a young lady to take an interest in good works.' He gazed at her admiringly, his grey eyes glinting from beneath his floppy copper-coloured locks.

'I, too, am involved with many charitable causes.'

'Indeed, Sir, I have heard much of your benevolence.'

'Then you may know of my plans to open a refuge for fallen women, here in Meryton?'

'That is most commendable. But it will be necessary, will it not, to find honest labour for the young ladies in question, or they may be tempted back to their licentious ways.'

Mr Darcy nodded in assent.

'I have considered that, Miss Bennet. I plan to open a tavern in the village, and the girls will work there as serving wenches. I shall call it ...'

He paused, and for a moment his smoky-grey eyes lingered over Lizzy's heaving bosom.

'... Hooters.

'An unusual name, Sir.'

'It is after my manservant, Mr Hooter, who shall be landlord there.'

'I see,' Elizabeth answered. 'And what brings you hither, Mr Darcy?'

'To Meryton?'

'To the haberdashers. We ladies are not accustomed to seeing gentlemen perusing ribbons and trimmings.'

Mr Darcy cast his eyes about the shop. 'I come here often, Miss Bennet,' he replied, with a hint of a smile. 'There are many accoutrements a gentleman of my nature requires for his private pursuits. See here,' he murmured, running one of his long index fingers down a length of grosgrain ribbon, suspended from a hook on the wall. 'This may prove useful.'

'You are preparing a collage, perhaps?' Elizabeth

enquired.

Mr Darcy's lips quirked up into a half-smile. 'No, not a collage, Miss Bennet,' he murmured.

'Perhaps trimming a pair of curtains?'

He chuckled softly, as if amused by some private joke. 'It is true that I favour a pair of neatly trimmed curtains.' His eyes pierced hers, and for a moment the air between them seemed to hum. *Had someone farted?*

'Yes, let us say that I am trimming some curtains. Perhaps you could assist me in choosing the materials?'

He proffered his arm and led her across to the counter, where numerous frills and furbelows and bolts of cloth were displayed.

'How may I oblige you, Mr Darcy, Miss Bennet?' asked the haberdasher, who, obviously being already acquainted with the former, was nonetheless bowing obsequiously low.

'Pray, give me four feet of your best horsehair braid,' Mr Darcy commanded. 'And ten feet of your finest curtain cord – it must be strong, mind you.'

Mr Darcy ran his eyes over the shelves. 'Fetch me some of that black leather-look fabric, there.'

'How much, Sir?'

'Oh, about enough to wrap once, tightly, about this young lady here.'

Black fabric and horsehair braid? These would certainly be distinctive curtains, Elizabeth thought. There was no denying Mr Darcy had unusual tastes.

'Will there be anything else, Sir?' asked the haberdasher.

'Just this curtain tie-back,' replied Mr Darcy, picking up a large golden tasselled braid. With a sudden 'whump!' he struck it, hard, against the wooden countertop. The whole counter trembled violently, and – although she could not discern why – so did Elizabeth's ladyparts.

'Is that all, Sir?'

'Let me see ...' Darcy was deep in thought for a moment. 'Do you have any dildos?'

Elizabeth's face blushed crimson. She lowered her eyes. This was insufferable! Why did Mr Darcy attempt to bring every conversation down to a crude level? To mortify her and shame her at every turn? How could he so cruelly disregard her feelings?

'You know why,' her Subconscious sighed. 'He went to private school.'

It was true! Poor Mr Darcy. How else could he possibly be, having been exposed to smut and salaciousness on a daily basis? Years of knob gags and lack of interaction with the opposite sex had moulded his character into a double-entendre-making, permanently smirking sex maniac, who simply could not help debasing himself.

The shopkeeper appeared to have been frozen to the spot by Mr Darcy's request.

'Do not trouble yourself, my good man,' the latter said, picking up a curtain rod with a decorative finial. 'This will do instead. Have everything delivered to Netherfield and charge it to my account.'

The haberdasher recovered his voice at last. 'As you wish, Mr Darcy. Good day, Sir.'

Elizabeth, who in her shame had turned her back on both gentlemen, was by now halfway to the door.

'Wait one moment, Miss Bennet,' Mr Darcy called. 'You must at least allow Taylor to escort you back to Longbourn.'

She whirled round in anger. 'Pray, do not go to any trouble on *my* account,' she retorted. 'I am able to negotiate my way from Meryton to my home quite satisfactorily. You may leave me alone hereafter. It would be far better than your continued attempts to harass and embarrass me whenever we have the misfortune to meet.'

Her words appeared to have a dramatic effect upon Mr Darcy. His lips de-quirked themselves at once, and his head ceased its cocking. Did she imagine it, or did his lower lip start to tremble, and his grey eyes grow dim with tears? Suddenly, he looked so young, so forsaken, that Elizabeth knew that if it was within her power, she wanted to save him. To save him from his dissolute life of butt plugs, handcuffs, golden showers, fisting, flogging, and anal probing. And to introduce him instead to a genteel world of découpage, shell collecting, lacework, needlepoint, and harpsichord recitals – gentle pastimes that would salve his damaged soul. But where to begin?

'If you won't go with Taylor, at least take hold of my knobkerry,' Mr Darcy said, proffering his cane. 'That way, if you are waylaid by ruffians, you will have no trouble beating them all off.'

Elizabeth's shoulders sagged. The road ahead, she realized, would be long and hard. A bit like an erect penis. *Holy crap, now she was doing it, too!* Mr Darcy was a dangerous influence indeed.

'We shall,' said Mr Bennet to his wife as they were at breakfast the next morning, 'have reason to expect an addition to our family party this evening.'

'Who do you mean, my dear? I know of no one who should happen to call in,' replied Mrs Bennet.

'The person of whom I speak is both known to us, and yet unknown.'

'Come, come,' cried Mrs Bennet impatiently. 'You speak in riddles, which is most out of character for you. Pray tell, who is this guest you speak of?'

'I have this morning received a letter from my cousin,

Mr Phil Collins, and he intends to pay us a visit this very afternoon.'

'*The* Phil Collins?' exclaimed his wife. 'Who used to be in Genesis? And is set to inherit Longbourn upon your death?'

'The very same!' Mr Bennet replied. 'It seems he has newly settled in Hertfordshire and comes hither to Longbourn with the intention of seeking a mistress.'

'One of my girls, having it off with Phil Collins!' cried Mrs Bennet. 'What a thought! Lady Lucas will be beside herself with envy! But come now, read out his letter, that we might all hear what he has to say.'

Mr Bennet duly obliged:

> *Dear Sir,*
> Having been ordained at Easter, I have been so fortunate as to be distinguished by the patronage of the Right Honourable Lady Catherine de Burgh, widow of the late Lord Chris de Burgh, whose bounty and beneficence has preferred me to the valuable rectory of this parish. Of Lady Catherine, you will have heard much, I do not doubt – of her affability, kindness, and magnificent embonpoint. She is indeed a remarkable woman. She'll get a hold on you, believe it. Like no other. And before you know it you'll be on your knees.
>
> But I digress. I have desire to make amends to your daughters for the circumstances of my being next in the entail of Longbourn estate, and with that in mind, I request the pleasure of waiting upon you and your family, this Monday 18 November at 4 o'clock. My intention, if it please you, is to pick one of your daughters to share my bedchamber, and possibly thereafter to enter into a three- to

five-year marriage followed by an acrimonious but financially advantageous divorce. It may seem hasty, but I believe you *can* hurry love, despite what Mama said.

Yours, Phil Collins

'He seems most conscientious and polite,' commented Mrs Bennet. 'You could do worse, girls, than hook up with a Grammy-award-winning rock god.'

'Nonetheless, there is something rather pompous in his style,' observed Elizabeth. 'The way he has managed to work in some of his song lyrics. And his obsequiousness regarding Lady Catherine. I wonder what kind of man he truly is?'

Elizabeth did not have to wait long for her answer. Mr Collins was punctual to his time, and was received with great politeness by the whole family. He was a small, balding man of about three score years, with a grave and formal manner, and little beady eyes. He had not long been seated before he complimented Mrs Bennet on having so fine a family of daughters. He found it impossible, he confessed, to choose between them, given that each clearly had her own merits.

'My Jane is easily the prettiest of them all,' remarked Mrs Bennet. 'Such fine strawberry-blonde locks! Such a magnificent rack! But alas! She is all but engaged to Mr Elliot Bingley, of Netherfield.'

'What of that one, with the slightly too-limpid eyes?' Mr Collins enquired, indicating Elizabeth, who was rolling about on the floor beside the fireplace, trying to force her unruly hair into a bonnet.

Mrs Bennet, who held her second-born the least dear of all her children, could not hide her delight. 'Now *there* is a suitable match, Mr Collins! My Lizzy will not mind that you have been married three times before, nor that it is rumoured you consider marriage to be a difficult proposition,' she said earnestly.

'I would need to ensure that Lady Catherine de Burgh, of course, approved of my choice,' said Mr Collins. 'As it happens, she is not well predisposed to romantic affiliations.'

'Why ever not, Mr Collins?' asked Mrs Bennet, who imagined all widows to be sex-starved nymphomaniacs.

'After the late Lord Chris de Burgh had a dalliance with the children's governess, she turned against romance. I know that she is adamant that her godson, Mr Fitzwilliam Darcy, should never marry.'

'Happily, he appears to be of the same mind,' broke in Elizabeth, who had caught the last few words of their discourse. 'Love does not appear to be one of his predilections.'

'Then he is very unlike me,' Lydia piped up, settling herself down upon Mr Collins's knee. '*I* think of little else.'

'For shame, Lydia, do not make a show of yourself,' her sister Mary hissed, through pursed lips.

'Why, Philip does not mind!' Lydia declared, rubbing Mr Collins's bald head affectionately. 'Now, Phil, tell us more about how you went Loco in Acapulco.'

Mr Collins declared his intention to stay the week, and over breakfast the next morning, the sisters were regaled with many tales of his former abode in Switzerland.

Lydia declared a desire to walk into Meryton, every sister agreed to accompany her, and Mr Collins insisted on attending them because he could 'feel something coming in the air tonight' and was anxious for their safety.

In pompous nothings on Mr Collins's side, and civil assents on that of his cousins, their time passed until they entered the village. Lydia and Kitty immediately cast about for soldiers, and their gaze soon settled upon a young officer with a most gentlemanly bearing. All the party were struck by the stranger's pleasing appearance, and upon enquiry, discovered him to be a Mr Whackem, a recent recruit to the militia.

Whackem was a tall, well-built fellow, with two silver hoop earrings glinting in his ears, and eyes of a fathomless deep blue. Elizabeth couldn't help but compare his red hair, tied back into a ponytail, with Mr Darcy's floppy copper locks. And neither could she help herself from trying to say, 'floppy copper locks' very fast, twenty times. It was surprisingly difficult.

Introductions were made, and soon the whole party was engaged in very agreeable conversation, when the sound of horses drew to their attention two riders approaching. It was Mr Bingley and Mr Darcy, the latter mounting a fine-looking chestnut mare. He deigned to acknowledge the company with a nod, but was suddenly arrested by the sight of the stranger, and Elizabeth, happening to see the countenances of both gentlemen, noticed that Mr Darcy's eyes grew dark and his jaw set firm, while Whackem visibly paled. After a few moments, Mr Whackem raised his hat, a gesture that Mr Darcy acknowledged by raising his middle finger and mouthing the word, 'Asshole.'

Whatever could it all mean? wondered Elizabeth. *Was there some enmity between the two gentlemen?*

Without another word, Mr Darcy wheeled his horse about and galloped back down the street, the way he had come. Mr Bingley appeared vexed.

'I *told* him to go to the water closet before we left,' he complained.

Mr Whackem, however, soon seemed to recover himself, and declared his intention to accompany the young ladies as far as the millinery shop.

'The militia is just a hobby for me,' he confided to Elizabeth as they walked along together. 'My true interest lies in books.'

'You love to read, Mr Whackem?' Elizabeth asked. 'So do I! Pray, which authors do you favour?'

'Reading is indeed a passion, Miss Bennet,' he replied, 'but it is to the *business* of books that I am most drawn. I have a small independent publishing company, Whackem Enterprises. We publish the *Whackem Official Sporting Guides*. You may know them better as the *Whackem Off* Series.

'Oh, but we have the *Whackem Off Guide to English Cricketers* at home!' Elizabeth cried. 'How fascinating that I have now met Mr *Whackem Off* himself!'

She pondered a moment. 'I always imagined, had I been born in some future time when young ladies might receive as rigorous an education as men, that I might have sought employment in the same sphere as yourself.'

'You might have wished to be a publishing executive?'

'A copywriter, perhaps, or a literary agent.'

Whackem's eyes lit up. 'Maybe you could consider doing a little proofreading for me?'

Elizabeth smiled. 'I could not possibly *work* for a living, Mr Whackem! I am far too busily engaged in pacing about the parlour, sticking pressed flowers in scrapbooks and embroidering cushion covers.' And yet she was not so lacking in pride as to deny that his talk of employment was flattering. The idea of enlisting her mind outside the domestic sphere appealed to her vanity, and, for a brief moment, she allowed herself to entertain the tantalizing thought.

The talk continued about Meryton, and forthcoming recitals and balls, but Elizabeth found herself chiefly wishing to hear what she could not hope to be told: the history of Whackem's acquaintance with Mr Darcy. Her curiosity was unexpectedly relieved, however, when Mr Whackem began the subject himself.

'We have a mutual acquaintance, I understand; one who abides at Netherfield.'

'You refer to Mr Darcy?'

'The very same. We are not on friendly terms. He has, in the past, used me very ill.'

Elizabeth's interest was at once piqued.

'I can never be in the company of Mr Darcy without being grieved by a thousand painful recollections,' Whackem continued. 'We grew up in the same household – my father managed the Pemberley estate – and he and I were boyhood companions, although I believe he disliked me even then. Later we were both sent to Beaton together.

'I had a teddy bear that I loved very much – Mrs Pickles was her name. She was given to me by Darcy's own father, the best man that ever lived. How I loved Mrs Pickles! She came with me everywhere.'

Elizabeth frowned. 'Forgive me, Mr Whackem, for interrupting your account, but I believe teddies have yet to be invented.'

'It is a deliberate anachronism, Miss Bennet,' said he, 'probably due to laziness on the part of the author. May we just gloss over it?'

'Of course. Please, continue.'

'One day, I woke to find Mrs Pickles was not in bed beside me as she was accustomed to be. She had quite vanished. How I searched in vain! Mrs Pickles was truly lost, it seemed, and my tears could not be stemmed. I was tender-hearted, you see, at that young age.'

'How old, may I ask, were you?' Elizabeth enquired.

'I was but fifteen.'

Elizabeth was deeply moved. The loss of a teddy bear, for one so young! It was sure to have scarred his character irreparably.

'At length,' Whackem continued, 'Mrs Pickles's whereabouts was discovered. It seems Fitzwilliam Darcy had taken her.' Whackem discreetly brushed away a tear.

'But what,' asked Elizabeth, after a pause, 'can have been his motive?'

'The pleasures of the flesh, Miss Bennet. Or in this case, the fluff. He had Mrs Pickles tied to his bedpost, whipped her, and used her sorely in a way that is not fit to describe in the presence of a young lady.'

Elizabeth let out a gasp. How could Mr Darcy be so cruel? To treat a soft toy in that way, it was truly monstrous!

'Mr Darcy declared Mrs Pickles to be his "submissive", and used his superior rank and connections to ensure that, from thereon, I had no claim upon my dearly loved toy. Mrs Pickles was kept in a makeshift sex dungeon under Darcy's bed, and flogged and debased on a daily basis. There was nothing I could do to save her.'

'Good heavens!' cried Elizabeth. 'How could this be disregarded? Why did you not seek legal redress?'

'I am a man of honour, Miss Bennet,' Mr Whackem said sadly. 'I would never knowingly do anything to sully the memory of Mr Darcy's late father, whom I held most dear. I thank God that he is dead and buried, and does not know of the shame his kinky son has brought upon the family name.'

'I had not thought Mr Darcy so bad as this,' Elizabeth confessed, 'although I admit, I do find him disturbingly oversexed. I imagined he would attempt to penetrate anything with a pulse, and may even harbour lustful

Fifty Shades of Mr Darcy

designs on melons, cream cakes, bolsters, and possibly
even garden furniture, but soft toys? Never! It is wicked
beyond belief!'

'You will understand now, Miss Bennet, why he and I
are careful to avoid each other?'

'Is is only natural, Mr Whackem,' commented Elizabeth.
'And you need have no fears on my account. He is not
welcome at Longbourn, and you are most unlikely to find
him there if you choose to visit us. Which I sincerely hope
you will.'

Mr Whackem smiled. 'I am gratified, Miss Bennet.
Come, let us have no more talk of Mr Darcy and his
abominable vices. My only consolation is that no woman
will ever have to suffer as Mrs Pickles did, as Mr Darcy will
never marry.'

'How can you be sure?'

'Lady Catherine de Burgh has forbidden it, and, for
reasons unknown, Mr Darcy would never defy her.'

'She has some influence over him, then?' Elizabeth
asked, puzzled. She could not imagine that a proud man
like Mr Darcy would take orders from a mere woman.

'Indeed, it seems so. She has known him since he was a
young boy. It is possible, I suppose, that he might harbour
some affection for her. She is, after all, a very handsome
woman.'

'Bitch troll!' snarled her Inner Slapper, most
unladylikely.

'Does Lady Catherine...' Elizabeth struggled to find the
appropriate words. 'How is she shaped? Is she tall or short?
Is her figure ample or slender? How would she compare,
for instance, to me?'

Mr Whackem glanced briefly at Elizabeth's modest
embonpoint and shrugged. 'I would say she definitely has
bigger knockers.'

The next day Elizabeth related to Jane what had passed between Mr Whackem and herself. Jane listened with astonishment – she knew not how to believe that Mr Darcy could be so unworthy of Mr Bingley's regard. Yet it was not in her nature to question the veracity of a young man of such amiable appearance as Mr Whackem. The possibility of Whackem having endured such torment was enough to interest all her tender feelings.

The sisters were interrupted in their conversation by the arrival of Carrotslime Bingley, who bore an invitation to yet another ball at Netherfield. This afforded Mrs Bennet ample opportunity to make many more testicle-themed double entendres, and the next week passed quickly in a whirl of bawdy jokes and the acquisition of new gowns and dancing slippers for all the Bennet sisters apart from Mary, who insisted that she found balls to be hot, sticky and unpleasant. Instead, she declared, she would stay at home and perfect her fingering with her music teacher, Mr Fiddler.

When at last Elizabeth entered the ballroom at Netherfield, she searched in vain for Mr Whackem among the cluster of red coats there assembled. She had the suspicion of his being purposely omitted for Mr Darcy's pleasure in Bingley's invitation to the officers. Lydia, who had already conversed with half the soldiers present, soon after delivered the news that Whackem was washing his hair that very evening, and would be unable to attend.

I do not imagine he would have chosen tonight to attend to his toilette, had he not wished to avoid a certain gentleman here, Elizabeth thought to herself.

She herself had dressed with more than usual care, borrowing Jane's plum-coloured silk gown, which accentuated her fine, lissome figure. It was a fact not lost on Mr Collins, who pronounced her to be almost as attractive as his beloved Lady Catherine de Burgh.

Mr Collins had secured the first two dances with Elizabeth, and for the latter they were dances of mortification and distress. Mr Collins, surprisingly for the former drummer with Genesis, displayed little rhythm, and often moved the wrong way without being aware of it. The moment of Elizabeth's release from him was ecstasy.

Discovering Charlotte Lucas in the orangery sneaking a cigarette, Elizabeth believed she had found both a refuge from the attentions of her stepfather's cousin, and a sympathetic ear.

'Oh Charlotte,' she sighed, 'I am beginning to think that I am being singled out among my sisters to be Phil Collins's mistress.'

'Would that be so disagreeable a thing, Lizzy?' Charlotte asked reasonably. 'Mr Collins is of no mean fortune, and with his back catalogue of hits, is sure to earn handsome royalties for many years to come.'

'That, I fear, is not enough to overcome my aversion to his company. I find him both foolish and tiresome. If I have to listen once more to his recollections of the Montreux Music Festival in '84, I declare I shall top myself!'

Charlotte smiled. 'You are too harsh, I think, Lizzy. I find him quite personable.'

'You surprise me, Charlotte! I had thought you more discerning.'

'At least you are attracting *some* male attention, however unwelcome,' countered Charlotte. 'I've had to dance with a yucca plant for the last two hours. Anyway, take a look under my petticoat. There should be a bottle of tequila somewhere.'

The young ladies' plan to get totalled on cheap booze

was soon thwarted, however, as Mr Collins, upon spying Elizabeth rummaging under her friend's gown, made his way out to the orangery to join them.

'I have found out,' said he, 'by a singular accident, that there is now in the room a close acquaintance of my patroness, Lady Catherine de Burgh. How wonderfully these things occur! I am now going to pay my respects to him, and trust he will excuse my not having done it before.'

'You intend to introduce yourself to Fitzwilliam Darcy?' asked Elizabeth.

'Indeed I am. He is Lady Catherine's godson, is he not?'

Elizabeth tried hard to dissuade him from such a scheme, assuring him that Mr Darcy would consider his addressing him when improperly attired in a 'Genesis Reunion World Tour' T-shirt as an impertinence rather than a compliment to his aunt. 'He is a proud man and a great stickler for appropriate dress,' Elizabeth advised him. 'At the very least put on your tailcoat.'

'Do not distress yourself, dear cousin,' Mr Collins reassured her. 'I have made a study of these points of etiquette, and when a man of the cloth, such as myself, is addressing the minor aristocracy, there is No Jacket Required.'

With that, he made his way across the room to the fireplace, where Mr Darcy stood prodding the coals with his poker.

Too mortified to witness the unfolding exchange, which would doubtless end in humiliation for Mr Collins and, by extension, to herself, Elizabeth contented herself with watching Jane and Mr Bingley. Their happiness and ease in each other's company was evident to all, and Elizabeth allowed herself to imagine Jane settled in that very house, in all the felicity that a marriage of true affection could bestow. Mrs Bennet evidently felt the same, as sidling up to Elizabeth, she said in a state of great animation: 'It goes well, does it not, for your sister? See how Mr Bingley rests his hand upon her buttock!'

In vain did Elizabeth endeavour to persuade her mother to describe the scene in a less audible whisper, for to her great distress, she sensed that the exchange was overheard by Mr Darcy, who had moved away from Mr Collins at the first opportunity and was now busy colour-coding a nearby fruit bowl.

'I am certainly not afraid to speak my mind in front of *him*,' her mother scolded, 'just because he has ten thousand a year! I dare say he thinks us a bunch of uncouth country bumpkins, but he would not look quite so superior if he knew that earlier, when he was not looking, I pissed in his glass of claret.'

Glancing sideways, Elizabeth discerned that Mr Darcy was not looking at her mother after all. Indeed, his smouldering grey eyes appeared to be trained, constantly, on her, following her every nuance of movement, every curve of her body. She squirmed under his scrutiny. It may have been Mr Darcy's persistent appraisal, or the heat of the room, the exertion of dancing or too many tequila slammers, but at length Elizabeth began to feel quite light-headed.

'I must go onto the balcony and take some air,' she declared to her mother, and, throwing open the doors, stepped into the clear, frosty night.

'Miss Elizabeth, are you not well?'

Mr Collins had appeared by her side, as if from nowhere, and his beady little eyes were boring into hers. 'May I be of assistance? Some water, perhaps?'

Elizabeth gathered some of the hair that had escaped from her chignon and tucked it back behind her ears. 'Pray, do not trouble yourself, Mr Collins. It is a momentary weakness, that is all.'

Mr Collins sprang forward so that his hands were upon her waist – they were drummer's hands, and surprisingly strong.

'Mr Collins! Whatever are you doing?'

'Oh Elizabeth...' Mr Collins stood up on his tiptoes and attempted to plant a kiss on her cheek.

'No, please do not!' Elizabeth protested. 'Stop, I beg you...'

'We could have a Groovy Kind of Love, Elizabeth,' Mr Collins whispered into her hair. 'Just let me kiss you...'

'I think the young lady said no!'

Holy hero! Mr Darcy was standing in the doorway, his rangy yet muscular physique almost blocking out the light from the ballroom beyond. His countenance betrayed a tumult of feelings: rage, passion, indigestion.

'Mr Darcy!' Mr Collins released Elizabeth at once. 'Miss Bennet was feeling unwell, and I was giving her succour.'

Mr Darcy's voice was clipped. 'If Miss Bennet is in need of succour, then *I* should be the person to administer it!'

'I do not need succour at all, I merely need fresh air,' Elizabeth said in an exasperated voice, bending over an aspidistra – she had an unsettling feeling that she might be sick. 'Please, I beg you both, leave me alone. I will be quite recovered in a moment.'

'You heard the lady,' Mr Darcy ordered.

'As you wish, Madam.' Giving a curt little bow, and a sideways glance at Elizabeth, Mr Collins retreated into the ballroom.

Mr Darcy strode across to Elizabeth and grasped her, tightly, by the buttocks.

'Are you quite well, Miss Bennet?' he asked anxiously, his eyes burning with concern.

'Quite well, thank you, Mr Darcy,' Elizabeth murmured

weakly. But just then, to her mortification and dismay, she was caught in a paroxysm of nausea and was violently sick all over Mr Darcy's calfskin boots. She was aware, as she was bending down, of Mr Darcy holding back her hair with tender care, and then, as she straightened up, of him braiding it deftly into plaits.

'Oooh, that's better,' he announced, clapping his hands. 'Pigtails!'

Looking upon her ashen countenance, he cocked his head to one side.

'Whatever are we to do with you, Miss Bennet?' he smirked. 'You are unused to alcohol. I take it you did not eat before you came here tonight? Perhaps I could get you a vol-au-vent?'

'I do not need to eat anything,' Elizabeth said impatiently. What was it with him and food?

'Pray, do not keep defying me, Miss Bennet!' Mr Darcy ordered. 'My God, you have no idea what it does to me...'

Seized by a sudden agitation, Mr Darcy strode about the balcony, his hands balled into fists at his side. After pacing for a minute or so, he turned to her and growled, 'Do you know what it did to me to see Phil Collins with his arms about you?'

Elizabeth was astounded, and immediately coloured.

'Put down those damn crayons and look at me!' Darcy commanded.

Elizabeth laid her colouring aside, and, tentatively, looked up to meet Mr Darcy's cold, penetrating gaze.

'You have no idea of the effect you have upon me, Miss Bennet,' Darcy said, running his hands through his copper hair. 'You do something to me. Something deep inside.'

'Please,' Elizabeth groaned, 'I have had my fill of song lyrics.'

Mr Darcy seemed to check himself. His face relaxed

and, straightening up, he held out his hand. 'Come...' he ordered. 'Dance with me.'

Elizabeth gazed up into those molten grey eyes, full of erotic promise and dark, dark desires. 'You still have sick on your boots,' she breathed. Mr Darcy shook the diced carrot from his feet with one sexy flick of each ankle. How masterful he was!

Elizabeth felt the eyes of all the assembled company upon her as Mr Darcy led her back into the ballroom. The fiddlers had just struck up a lively tune, and he bowed low, his lips quirking into an amused half-smile.

'Shall we jig, Miss Bennet?'

Although Elizabeth's every inclination was to decline, to retreat to the safety of the balcony, she felt inexorably drawn to him, like a mouse is lured by a hunk of cheese towards a steel trap. Into what dangers would her desire for this cheesy hunk lead her?

Curtseying, she took Mr Darcy's hand, and allowed herself to be chasséd across the room. *He dances so beautifully,* thought Elizabeth, as Mr Darcy performed a neat fleuret.

Her head still swimming from her tequila binge, Elizabeth was soon lost in the music. It was hypnotic: the drummers drummed, the flautists flauted, and the fiddlers kept on fiddling – despite many polite requests to do it in private. Mr Darcy moved sensuously to the rhythm, moving his hips in snake-like patterns, grinding his body against Elizabeth's and then pulling away – teasing, tantalizing her until she wished for more. As the music reached a crescendo, he span away across the dance floor, performed two high kicks followed by a shoulder shimmy, and then landed – with a high-pitched squeal – in the splits.

'Don't say it,' she muttered to her Gaydar.

Mr Darcy rose languidly from the floor, and made his way through the throng to Elizabeth's side, never once taking his eyes from hers. She could smell his by-now-familiar leathery scent wafting across the dance floor as he moved, and her insides performed a somersault, with her kidneys ending up somewhere underneath her bladder. There was no denying her powerful attraction to him. *Dancing, walking, talking – was there anything Mr Darcy didn't do sexily?* she wondered.

'You look faint, Miss Bennet,' he said in a voice tinged with anxiety. 'I trust you are not feeling unwell again?' He guided her towards a chair. 'Wait there, I shall fetch you some hors d'oeuvre.' Before she could speak he was away again, striding purposefully through the dancers as they attempted to do-si-do in formation, scattering them hither and thither and accidentally kicking Carrotslime Bingley in the shins. *Jeez, he even collected snacks sexily*, thought Elizabeth.

At that moment, she was distracted by the sound of giggling from underneath the console table to her right. Curious, she lifted up the floral swags and muslin drapery with which it was decorated and peered underneath. In the darkness she could just make out two figures, evidently a man and a woman, closely entwined.

'Why, whatever are you doing there?' she enquired.

The figures immediately sprang apart. Elizabeth stared in astonishment as the young lady hastily adjusted the buttons of her gown.

Her companion reddened.

'Miss Bennet.' Mr Collins nodded gravely.

'And *Charlotte*?' Elizabeth gasped. 'Is that you?'

Charlotte Lucas, for it was indeed she, looked up at Elizabeth with a grin that lit up her potato-like face.

'Have you lost something?' Elizabeth asked, uncertain

as to why her stepfather's cousin and her closest friend were scrabbling under a table like kitchen mice.

'Indeed I have, Elizabeth,' Charlotte replied with a triumphant smile. 'My virtue.'

To be deflowered, by Phil Collins, under a table at a party! This was unwelcome news indeed! Whatever was Charlotte thinking?

'Charlotte! I confess I am shocked! I had not thought you would give up your virtue so easily.'

'Oh, get real, Elizabeth,' Charlotte sighed. 'It's easy for you to say. You're gorgeous. I, on the other hand, look like the back end of a coach-and-four. We both know I've been lucky to get rid of it at all.'

Poor Mr Collins was by now the colour of Elizabeth's gown. 'Please . . . this is a most indelicate situation. I have taken advantage of Mr Bingley's hospitality most grievously. You must forgive me, ladies...' He attempted to scrabble to his feet, but only succeeded in hitting his bald head upon the underside of the table.

'But Charlotte, did you even ever consider the consequences?' Elizabeth said with passion. 'What would happen if you got with child?'

Mr Collins turned an even deeper shade of puce. 'Please rest assured, you need have no worries on that score,' he mumbled, his eyes fixed upon the floorboards. 'I Missed Again.'

Elizabeth was not sure whether to be insulted or amused. Not an hour before, Mr Collins had been making protestations of love to her, and assuring her of the strength of his affections in no uncertain terms. Yet here he was, getting his leg over Charlotte Lucas under a console table. She felt no jealousy, however, only relief; if Mr Collins truly had transferred his affections to Charlotte, she would no longer have to entertain the prospect of becoming his mistress.

She heard footsteps approaching behind her and hurriedly dropped the tablecloth, anxious that her best friend's disgrace remain undiscovered for at least a few more moments.

A husky, familiar voice murmured, 'Titbits?'

She whirled round and was once again caught in the mesmerizing gaze of Mr Fitzwilliam Darcy.

'If you must demean me by calling me by a pet name,' she declared with what she hoped was hauteur, 'I would rather it was anything but *that*.'

Mr Darcy seemed amused. His grey eyes danced with merriment as he held out a plate laden with sugared almonds, sugared plums and deep-fried cheese balls.

'I was referring to *these* titbits, Miss Bennet.' He looked so smug, so pleased with himself, Elizabeth was once again roused to anger.

'What is it with you and food?' she burst out. *Damn her cheap stays, they were ridiculously flimsy!* Blushing, she tucked her bosom back into place.

'What is it with you and food?' she repeated, this time without bursting out.

Mr Darcy's expression darkened. 'Do not ask me that, Miss Bennet.'

'I just did.'

'Believe me, you do not want to know the answer.'

'I do. That's why I asked you.'

Mr Darcy's grey eyes had lost their warmth now, and turned dark as the blackest sea. His palm was twitching, as if it had a life of its own. *What was going through his mind?* Elizabeth wondered. *Which of his fifty shades was she witnessing?* Suddenly, Mr Darcy's palm lifted high in the air, quivered there for one tantalizing moment, then swept down and landed – *thwack!* – upon Elizabeth's reticule.

Her whole body shuddered, both with dismay and shame.

'*That* is what you get for defying me!' Mr Darcy growled, and with that, he turned upon his heel and stalked away without looking back.

Elizabeth found herself unable to speak, so badly shaken was she by the turn of events. Her legs felt suddenly weak and, putting out a hand to steady herself, she sank onto a nearby chair. 'Thank heavens I brought my reticule out with me tonight,' she shuddered, 'or that smack would have landed right on my beaver.'

Thus it was settled. Charlotte was to marry Phil Collins. The arrangement would come to an end in a few years, when Mr Collins met someone younger and prettier, and as part of the settlement, Charlotte would receive Hunsford Priory.

Elizabeth found it hard to reconcile herself to so unsuitable a match. It would be impossible for her friend to be happy, she believed, with Phil Collins pawing at her day and night.

'But I am not like you, Elizabeth,' Charlotte countered. 'I have not the advantage of your good looks, your wit. I just need to get out of Meryton. It's dead round here.'

'And you believe sharing a bed with Mr Collins is a small price to pay?'

'I would shag the Prince Regent if I had to.'

Charlotte could not be swayed, and so Elizabeth made a strong effort of will to reconcile herself to the match. Charlotte's departure for Hunsford was imminent – Mr Collins being so eager to introduce her to Lady Catherine de Burgh – and with the prospect of losing her close friend, Elizabeth turned increasingly to Jane.

Her sister's happiness was a cause of great anxiety for Elizabeth, who noted that Mr Bingley had called only once in the week following the ball. Now they heard he would be absent from Longbourn for another week, having gone to London on business with Mr Darcy – a fact that caused Elizabeth much relief.

'You have not put out enough!' Mrs Bennet berated Jane. 'Gentlemen wish to feel that all is not hopeless in a courtship. A sneaky feel behind the shrubbery, or a glimpse of nipple in the rose garden, is enough to keep their ardour aflame.'

Kitty and Lydia shared their mother's concerns, and advised Jane on the gown-slippage techniques that ensured they remained popular among the officers of the Meryton militia.

Only Mary was disinterested. 'Please, do not discuss affairs of the heart in front of me,' she declared. 'I have little interest in such matters. If most young ladies occupied themselves with books and music, as I do, the world would doubtless be a happier, less discordant place.'

Her younger sisters scorned her, but Mary paid little heed, and threw herself more vigorously into her music lessons with Mr Fiddler. There was no denying that under his tutelage her fingering had improved exponentially, and he himself evidently took pleasure in teaching her, and frequently left the house quite flushed with satisfaction.

While Mr Bingley and Mr Darcy were absent, Mr Whackem was a more frequent visitor to Longbourn. His easy charm and beguiling good looks made a favourable impression upon Mrs Bennet, who declared him the most amiable young man of their acquaintance. Her husband was most appreciative of the many freebies Mr Whackem was wont to bring along from his publishing company: indeed, he spent many happy hours poring over *Steamy Pumping Action: Piston Engines of Industrial England.* Meanwhile, Lydia and Kitty professed themselves delighted by Mr Whackem's gifts of *Rockin' those Stockings!* and *Bootylicious Bonnets.*

Whackem singled out Elizabeth at every occasion, and the pair made it their habit to take a turn about the formal garden while discussing their many topics of mutual interest. Mr Darcy was occasionally the subject of their discourse, in particular, his insufferable arrogance and insatiable sex mania.

On one bracing January morning, Elizabeth and Whackem were partaking of their usual perambulation, when Mr Whackem raised the issue of Mr Bingley's intentions towards Jane.

'It is a delicate issue, I know,' he declared, 'but I cannot help but wonder whether Mr Darcy has had something to do with Mr Bingley's apparent coolness towards your sister.'

'Mr Darcy?' cried Elizabeth, plunging her hands deeper into her muff, in order to ward off the cold. 'What ever would it have to do with him?'

'He is, as you know, a cold and unfeeling creature,' Whackem replied. 'He hates to see happiness in others, and especially in those who value finer feelings such as love, honour and trust, and do not share his dark predilections.'

'You are too harsh, I think. Mr Darcy has his faults – indeed, they are myriad – but to wilfully separate Jane from Mr Bingley? Even he would not sink so low.'

'Then what lies behind Bingley's current indifference?' Whackem asked. 'You tell me he has corresponded with Jane but once this past fortnight.'

Elizabeth was silent for a few moments while she weighed up Mr Whackem's words. She was loath to believe so badly of Mr Darcy, even though she was still not yet recovered from the blow he had landed on her reticule.

'I believe Carrotslime Bingley is at fault,' she declared. 'Her intention is for Mr Bingley to marry Mr Darcy's sister, thus hoping that with their two families so entwined, Mr Darcy will marry *her*.'

'And what of you, Miss Bennet?' Mr Whackem asked, looking at her askance through ginger eyelashes.

'Me, Mr Whackem?' Elizabeth laughed. 'Why, I do not think of matrimony at all!'

'You can think of no one who you would wish to marry?'

Elizabeth frowned. 'Did you just say "*who* you would wish to marry? It should be "*whom*".'

Far from being abashed by her perspicacity, Mr Whackem appeared delighted.

'You are correct, Miss Bennet!' he exclaimed. 'I threw in that little grammatical error to see whether you would pick up on it, and I am gratified that it did not pass your notice.'

'You are testing my grammar, Mr Whackem?'

'You seem to have an aptitude for it, Miss Bennet. I would bet ten guineas that you would be able to distinguish the proper use of the colon and the semicolon.'

'Surely most young ladies would know that?' Elizabeth said, shivering a little in the frosty air. Mr Whackem appeared not to notice. *How unlike Mr Darcy,* Elizabeth thought. *He would have seen to it that I was smothered in muffs by now.*

'You would be surprised, Miss Bennet,' Whackem sighed. 'Most young ladies are wantonly ill-educated. It is most vexing trying to find copy-editors with the necessary skills.'

Was he about to propose work again? Elizabeth remained silent, conscious that any response might serve to give him encouragement.

Whackem appeared to sense her reticence, and, walking at a brisk pace back towards the house, they soon began discussing the many benefits of outdoor exercise. Lydia was waiting for them at the door.

'Lizzy, you have had Mr Whackem to yourself for quite long enough,' she complained. 'Mary is studying, Kitty is at her toilette, and I long for conversation.' She seized Whackem's arm. 'Let us walk along the path towards the rose garden,' she said brightly, 'and you can tell me all about how you came to be a lieutenant.'

Whackem appeared momentarily disappointed to leave Elizabeth's side, but his handsome countenance soon recovered its usual attentive guise, and he allowed himself to be led away by a chattering Lydia. Elizabeth watched them round the corner to the orchard, and heard Whackem's voice cut through the frosty air. 'Pray tell, Lydia, how do you suppose you spell "lieutenant"?'

February took Elizabeth to Hunsford, to visit Charlotte and Phil Collins. The plan had been laid some weeks before, and Elizabeth had not at first thought very seriously of going thither, but Charlotte, she soon found, was depending on her presence.

Avoiding Mr Darcy was now Elizabeth's main intent, and a stay at Hunsford would be exactly what was needed to distract her. Besides, absence had increased her desire of seeing Charlotte again, and she found herself looking favourably upon the scheme.

The journey, some twenty-four miles, passed pleasantly enough, and when the carriage left the high road for the lane to Hunsford, Elizabeth was eager to gain sight of the Parsonage. Soon there behoved into view, at the end of a long gravel path, a small yet elegant building of pale stone, with windows and a door and some fancy eighteenth-century features that the author didn't have sufficient architectural knowledge to describe.

The inhabitants of the house had all emerged to mark her arrival.

'Lizzy! I said you'd come!' smiled Charlotte. 'Mr Collins declared that it was Against All Odds, but *I* did not agree.'

Charlotte did not appear diminished from having to have sex with Phil Collins every night; indeed, she seemed to glow with inner happiness.

'How well you look!' commented Elizabeth, as the two friends walked arm in arm into the lobby. 'Marriage seems to suit you very well, Charlotte. I trust you find Mr Collins an agreeable husband?'

Charlotte grimaced. 'He is out in his stu-stu-studio every night, playing the drums,' she said quietly, so as not to be overheard. 'But thankfully, that gives me time for a little liaison of my own, with Mellors the gardener.'

'Mellors?'

'Yes, he is a man from the village – a very rough type – who comes over whenever my box needs to be trimmed. Oh, Lizzy, I think he is in love with me, and I with him! He is such a wonderful listener, and I have so much I want to say to him.' She gave a girlish laugh. 'He calls me Lady Chattery.'

'No, this will not do!' exclaimed Elizabeth, vexed beyond all measure. 'Two books colliding is enough! It is too, too confusing. I beg you, Charlotte, do not mention Mellors again.'

Charlotte was taken aback by the vigour of Elizabeth's protestations. 'You are tired from your journey, perhaps?' she suggested. 'Come, let me show you to your room, and then perhaps you will tell me your impressions of Mr

Fitzwilliam Darcy. Lord knows we hear of little else from Lady Catherine.'

When Elizabeth had rested awhile, Mr Collins invited her to take a stroll in the gardens. They were large and well laid out, and more than once she was required to stop and admire his peonies. He spoke at length of the affability of the Hunsford populace, the pleasing aspects of the surrounding countryside, and especially the many estimable qualities of his neighbour, Lady Catherine de Burgh of Rosings Park.

'You will have the honour of meeting Lady Catherine tomorrow night,' Mr Collins informed her, 'when we are all invited to dine at Rosings.'

'Lady Catherine was a great friend of Fitzwilliam Darcy's mother, was she not?'

'That is true, Miss Bennet,' Mr Collins replied, clearly delighted in her interest, feigned or otherwise. 'They were both beauty therapists originally, I believe. Lady Catherine owns a chain of beauty spas, which have brought her great wealth. And of course, she married exceedingly well.'

'Ah yes,' mused Elizabeth, 'to international MOR star Chris de Burgh. If only we could all be so fortunate.'

In truth, she had little desire to meet Lady Catherine. After all, it was under her influence that Fitzwilliam Darcy had grown into the smirking sex pervert he was today. And yet her curiosity was roused. Lady Catherine was by all accounts a powerful woman, and a handsome one, and Elizabeth had many unanswered questions. Chief among them, which of them *did* have the bigger bubbies?

Mr Collins could talk of little else all day but their forthcoming visit to Rosings Park that evening. When the time arrived for Charlotte and Elizabeth to attend to their toilette, he came to their rooms several times, ostensibly to advise them not to keep Lady Catherine waiting, but in actuality to try to catch a glimpse of Elizabeth's undergarments.

'I beg you to excuse my husband's sex-pestery,' Charlotte said apologetically when Mr Collins had finally gone downstairs to await the carriage. 'I'm afraid the prospect of an evening in Lady Catherine's company invariably has a stimulating effect upon his natural urges.'

'In that respect he is not alone,' replied Elizabeth, thinking of Mr Darcy's unwillingness to defy his godmother. 'She appears to exert a powerful hold over men.'

Charlotte nodded. 'It's true, she is a beauty. You will see for yourself soon enough. But she is also a *total bitch*.'

'Really?'

'Try not to anger her; she has a wicked temper. I said something she didn't like last time we were there, and she nearly twisted my nipples off.'

Presently the carriage arrived and the party set out from the Parsonage, up the long, winding driveway that cut through Rosings Park and led to the house itself. It was a grand, imposing building of the old style, with some windows, some walls and a door blah di blah. Ascending the steps, they followed the servants into the lobby, and from thence to the room where Lady Catherine was waiting for them.

Elizabeth's heart was in her mouth. She swallowed, hard, and it slipped back down. It was the last thing she needed, she thought anxiously, on the back of her kidney/bladder problem, which still hadn't quite righted itself.

Standing in the centre of the room, one spike-heeled boot pressing down on an unfortunate footman's head, was a tall, shapely woman in a full leather gimp suit, brandishing a long leather whip. She turned to glare at the party. 'Did I say you could come in?' she snarled.

Mr Collins cringed. 'N... no, no, your ladyship,' he stammered. 'Please accept our humble apologies. Should we, um, go back out again?'

Lady Catherine took her boot off her servant's head. 'You may go now, Saunders,' she said coldly. 'Let me not catch you whistling again, or it's the thumbscrews for you.' The servant scrabbled to his feet and backed hurriedly out of the room, muttering apologies all the way.

Lady Catherine turned her attention to the newcomers. 'Well, do not just stand there! Come forward!' she demanded. As the party tentatively advanced, she pulled off her gimp mask, and a cascade of pale-blonde hair tumbled down past her shoulders. She was a magnificent-looking woman, despite her advanced years, and her bubbies, Elizabeth noted sourly, were indeed far larger than her own.

'You!' Lady Catherine exclaimed, pointing the whip directly at Elizabeth. 'What is your name?'

Elizabeth gave a brief curtsey. 'Elizabeth Bennet, your ladyship.'

'And where do you reside?'

'At Longbourn, in Hertfordshire.'

Lady Catherine wrinkled her exquisite nose. 'Hmmm, you are sorely in need of a makeover. Let me see...' She stepped forward and grasped Elizabeth's chin, hard, turning it this way and that with her leather-clad hand. 'Eyebrow threading. Upper-lip bleach. And for pity's sake, do something about those open pores.'

Abruptly, she let go, leaving Elizabeth feeling bruised

and humiliated, and turned to Mr Collins.

'And what time, pray, do you call this? You are *three and a half minutes late.*'

Mr Collins blanched. 'Forgive us, Lady Catherine, the ladies and their toilette...'

'Be silent!' commanded Lady Catherine. 'You are a very naughty boy! What are you?'

'A very naughty boy?' Mr Collins said in a small voice, visibly cringing.

'That's right. And what do I do to very naughty boys?'

'Punish them?' squeaked Mr Collins.

'That is correct. Go over to my armoire, Mr Collins, and select from within it the largest butt plug you can find. You shall sit upon it while we dine, until I am satisfied you have learnt your lesson.'

Elizabeth gasped. Charlotte lowered her eyes in mortification. But Mr Collins's expression, perversely, was bright-eyed, even eager.

'Thank you, Lady Catherine, it is an honour,' he said, bowing low.

'Come, ladies, we shall take our repast,' announced Lady Catherine. 'Join us, Mr Collins, when you have arranged yourself.'

She strode off towards a door in the corner of the room, her gimp suit creaking and her spike heels clicking on the wooden floorboards.

'We must follow at once,' hissed Charlotte, 'or risk displeasing her.'

'What a bitch troll she is,' Elizabeth hissed back. 'I don't care whether she does own a string of top beauty salons, I'm going to tell her what I think of her.'

'Pray don't, Lizzy,' Charlotte begged. 'We have asked for her permission to hold a music festival, Philstock, on her land, and if she refuses, we will lose a considerable investment.'

Elizabeth sighed. 'Then for the sake of our friendship, I must hold my tongue. But it will not be easy.'

'Where are you, lazy trollops?' Lady Catherine's voice boomed from the next room. 'Bestir yourselves!'

Elizabeth followed Charlotte into the dining room and immediately her jaw dropped in astonishment. *What kinky fuckery was this?* Several chairs were laid out in the centre of the room, and before each was a servant, kneeling on all fours. Lady Catherine was seated in the grandest chair, and had rested her wine glass upon a buxom serving girl's buttocks.

'Mrs Jenkinson!' Lady Catherine called, and from a side door there emerged a frail-looking maidservant, almost bent double with age, wearing a leather harness and bridle. A pony's tail was attached to the back of her gown.

'Yes, Mistress?' she enquired, the metal bit grinding audibly against her teeth.

'Bring the soup!'

Mrs Jenkinson shuffled off, her tail swinging limply behind her.

Holy crap, what was this place? Elizabeth could only shudder that Fitzwilliam Darcy had fallen into Lady Catherine's clutches at such a tender age; there was no humiliation, no degradation that was not on display here. Tentatively, she took a seat in front of a young footman, who was wearing nothing but leather trousers and nipple clamps. Mrs Jenkinson laid a bowl of soup and a spoon upon the footman's hairy back.

'Well, eat up,' Lady Catherine barked. 'This will soon go cold.' She slurped her soup loudly.

'Do you play, Miss Bennet?' she suddenly asked. 'A young lady should most definitely play the pianoforte.'

'A little,' Elizabeth replied, 'although I confess I have not much natural talent.'

'That is most displeasing!' Lady Catherine declared, her icy blue eyes narrowing. 'You shall play for me later, and if I judge your performance to be lacking in skill, I shall have to chastise you.'

Elizabeth felt her skin prickling. *How dare she?*

'With respect, Lady Catherine, how do you intend to do that?'

'With ten lashes upon your derriere, of course.'

'And if I am resistant to the idea of punishment?'

Lady Catherine eyed her appraisingly. 'You are defiant, Miss Bennet. Perhaps, in your case, ten lashes will not suffice. Perhaps I shall have to leash you to my pony trap beside Jenkinson, and have you pull me about the grounds.'

'Go fu...' Elizabeth began, but at that very moment, there emerged in the doorway a very uncomfortable-looking Mr Collins.

'I do so hope I have not kept you all waiting,' he said obsequiously, shuffling gingerly across the room like a man three times his age. He lowered himself into a seat, wincing. Jenkinson laid out a bowl of soup on the servant in front of him.

'None for me, please.'

'You are full, Mr Collins?' Lady Catherine asked, her cold eyes glinting with malice.

'Painfully so, Lady Catherine.'

'I insist that you partake of the next course. It is roast goose,' she commanded. 'Although on this occasion, given the circumstances, I shall allow you to forgo the stuffing.'

The first fortnight of Elizabeth's visit soon passed away. She and the Collinses dined four more times at Rosings, each occasion being more deplorable than the last. Lady Catherine appeared in various guises: sometimes in her gimp suit, sometimes in a red leather corset, and, on the fourth evening, sporting an eyewateringly huge strap-on dildo – a sight that caused Mr Collins almost to fall into a faint. At that particular dinner, Lady Catherine announced that they were soon to be graced with a visit from her godson, Mr Darcy, a prospect that gave her great joy. Mr Darcy, she pointed out, could never do enough to please her.

Hearing the news, Elizabeth was overwhelmed by conflicting emotions. The prospect of being in such close proximity to Fitzwilliam Darcy alarmed her. And yet undeniably, he thrilled her in a way that her usual pleasures such as tinkling her harpsichord could never do. Would he launch another assault on her reticule? Her Inner Slapper certainly hoped that he would.

Mr Darcy's arrival at Rosings was quickly noted by Mr Collins, who had witnessed the gentleman's carriage approaching Rosings Park when he was in the garden watering his peonies. That very afternoon, Mr Darcy arrived at Hunsford to pay his respects. A sharp rap on the door announced his arrival, and shortly afterwards he was shown into the parlour, where Charlotte and Elizabeth were at their needlepoint.

'How do you do, Miss Bennet, Mrs Collins.'

Mr Darcy bowed low, his breeches stretching tight over his taut buttocks. A lock of curly copper hair fell in front of his eyes. *Holy hornbag, he was so hot!*

Why do I keep uttering profanities whenever I encounter Fitzwilliam Darcy? pondered Elizabeth. *It is so out of character for me, for crap's sake. Holy crap, I just did it again!*

Mr Darcy took a seat beside Elizabeth. 'You are well, Miss Bennet? Have you been eating heartily?'

Elizabeth could not resist toying with him, as he had so often toyed with her. 'I skipped breakfast this morning,' she declared, and immediately noticed his jaw tighten.

'Then it is well that I have a baguette in my pocket,' he countered, reaching into his breeches and pulling out a thick French stick. 'Would you oblige me with a nibble?'

Once again, Elizabeth was conscious of a stirring in her nether regions. What was it about this arrogant billionaire that attracted her so?

'Your baguette looks most enticing, but I rarely eat at this time of day. I cannot be tempted!'

'A banana, then?' Mr Darcy suggested, reaching into his other pocket. 'Or this German sausage?'

Elizabeth felt her blood beginning to heat up her cheeks.

'It is kind of you, Mr Darcy, to be so desirous of my well-being, but I assure you, nothing shall pass my lips until luncheon.'

Mr Darcy's eyes flashed in anger. 'Very well, Miss Bennet,' he said darkly. 'I see you are defiant. Be assured, if you were a guest in *my* house and refused my hospitality, I should see to it that you were chastised.'

For a moment he sounded so like Lady Catherine that Elizabeth was at a loss for words. Then, recovering her composure, she declared, 'You are too harsh, Mr Darcy. If you were ever a guest at Longbourn and found my syllabubs, say, or my hare pie were not to your liking, I should endeavour not to hold it against you.'

Mr Darcy leant forward and held her in a penetrating gaze. 'You and I are very different, Miss Bennet,' he murmured. 'You see, I would find your hare pie *quite delicious*, and would be sure to enjoy it morning, noon and night. I would dive into it at breakfast, luncheon and dinner, then I would ask for seconds.'

'I would find your appetite most gratifying, I am sure,' blushed Elizabeth. 'But some of us are less gluttonous than others. I myself am content with the occasional muffin.'

Mr Darcy smiled lasciviously. 'Then we are in agreement at last, Miss Bennet,' he smirked.

'Um, should I leave the room?' asked Charlotte.

'No need, Mrs Collins,' said Mr Darcy, rising from his chair. 'I must depart. Lady Catherine urged me to hurry back; we are going riding – hard – together. She is to send a carriage for you at eight,' he continued, 'in order that you may dine with us tonight.' Then, addressing Elizabeth directly: 'I am so glad that the two of you have met at last.'

'I'm sure we shall be great friends,' said Elizabeth with a tight smile.

'Really?' Mr Darcy's face lit up. 'I do hope so. She is a remarkable woman.' With a bow he departed, and Elizabeth turned back to her needlepoint. She frowned. She would have to unpick it and start again. 'There's no place like home bitch troll bitch troll bitch troll bitch troll' would not look quite right on a cushion cover.

At the proper hour Elizabeth and Mr and Mrs Collins arrived at Rosings, to be told Lady Catherine was at her toilette and would not keep them waiting long. A footman led them into a small, comfortable parlour, tastefully decorated with black leather furnishings and paintings of goats being sodomized by demons. Suddenly, Charlotte let out a cry of alarm, and, following her gaze, Mr Collins and Elizabeth noticed a figure kneeling in the corner of the room, his eyes downcast, clad only in leather hotpants and a studded collar: Mr Darcy! Elizabeth gaped at him. *Jeez, he was ripped!*

'Pray, what are you doing down there, Mr Darcy?' she gasped. 'For shame, get up and put on some clothes.'

'He is *not* to move!'

Lady Catherine appeared in the doorway, her impressive leather-clad bosom halfway across the threshold and her skintight catsuit creaking menacingly.

'Mr Darcy has displeased me, and this is his punishment.'

Mr Darcy remained motionless. *It's almost as if he's in a trance*, thought Elizabeth. *What power Lady Catherine has over him! How cruel and domineering she is!*

'I am sure your ladyship knows best,' Mr Collins simpered, bowing obsequiously. 'It reminds me of a Genesis tour in '78, when I had to send Mike Rutherford to Coventry for–'

'But to humiliate him so!' Elizabeth burst out. 'Can it truly be justified?'

Charlotte tugged at Elizabeth's sleeve. 'Please hold your tongue, Lizzy,' she whispered. 'Think of Philstock ...'

Lady Catherine swept over to Mr Darcy and seized him by the hair. 'Get up!' she ordered. 'Our guests need some peanuts.'

'Yes, Mistress,' Darcy intoned in a low voice, rising to his feet. Making his way over to a sideboard, never once lifting his eyes, he took down two china dishes and made his way over to Mr Collins.

'Will his punishment last long?' the latter asked, seizing a handful of Mr Darcy's nuts.

'Until I am satisfied,' replied Lady Catherine.

Elizabeth watched Mr Darcy as he moved wordlessly about the room. He looked so different – so young, so vulnerable, so broken. Damn Lady Catherine! How could she have dragged him into the dark, twisted world she inhabited? She, Elizabeth, would show him there was another way. An afternoon of découpage, a duet upon the dulcimer ... Such diversions could surely lead even the most damned soul towards the light.

'Sit!' Lady Catherine barked, and Mr Darcy returned to his place beside the doorway and knelt, wordlessly, once again.

Lady Catherine turned to Elizabeth. 'Now, Miss Bennet, I insist upon hearing you play the pianoforte. Mr Darcy shall turn the pages for you, with his teeth.'

The evening continued in excruciating fashion, Mr Darcy performing the work of a humble servant, and Elizabeth and the Collinses in a constant state of mortification and distress. The only person who enjoyed herself was Lady Catherine, who seemed to delight in both Mr Darcy's humiliation and her guests' discomfiture. Try as Elizabeth might to turn the conversation towards innocent pastimes, such as flower arranging, Lady Catherine would insist upon turning it back to subjects such as fisting and genital clamping. And not once did Mr Darcy so much as glance at Elizabeth, despite her best efforts to catch his eye.

'She is the most interesting woman, is she not?' declared Mr Collins as the carriage journeyed back to Hunsford. 'Unusual hobbies, though, I admit.'

'I confess, I find her taste in dress a little outlandish,' commented Charlotte. 'I had never imagined that it was possible for a lady to wear earrings *down there*.'

Mr Collins beamed at Elizabeth. 'And how, cousin, do you find Lady Catherine? She seems to take a particular interest in you.'

'She is a complete and utter bi...' Elizabeth began, but Charlotte's pleading look arrested her mid-sentence. 'She is,' she began more diplomatically, 'a law unto herself'.

'And a slag,' her Inner Slapper added.

But chief among the impressions that particular evening at Rosings had left upon Elizabeth was her fresh determination to save Mr Darcy from his errant ways. The burden weighed heavily upon her, and she slept fitfully that night, dreaming of firm buttocks in leather hotpants, and scratching out Lady Catherine's eyes.

Over the next few weeks, as Elizabeth's sojourn at Hunsford continued, Mr Darcy was a frequent visitor to the Parsonage. In fact, he had a habit of appearing when Elizabeth least expected it. Once he surprised her in the garden when she was trimming Charlotte's box; several times she stumbled across him in the woods – though quite what he was doing concealed in a pile of leaves was beyond her – and he even tapped upon the window of her bedroom when she was using the chamber pot, ostensibly to talk about new harnesses and fittings for his pony trap. It was all beginning to have a detrimental effect upon Elizabeth's nerves.

'You always come unexpectedly!' she accused him when next they met, in the lane behind the Parsonage.

Mr Darcy's eyes narrowed. 'Who have you been talking to?' he said in a low voice.

'I mean to say,' Elizabeth explained, 'that you never give notice of your visits.'

'Why Miss Bennet, I like to pop up and surprise you,' he said with a sly smile. 'Indeed, I am popping up right now as we speak.'

Their talk was usually of Longbourn, Pemberley or the weather, and Elizabeth did not feel she could raise the matter of what she had seen on her last visit to Rosings. Why did Lady Catherine have such power over Mr Darcy? He had money of his own, property and prestige, and, she was informed, a joint share in her beauty spa business.

Why did he need to debase himself in such a fashion? And those leather hotpant ... She could not quite erase the memory from her mind.

Late one morning, a few days before she was due to depart, Elizabeth was roused by the sound of the doorbell. Her spirits were made a little anxious by the idea of it being Lady Catherine, who had threatened to come down and take tea with her. But this idea was soon banished, and her spirits were very differently affected, when, to her utter amazement, she saw Mr Darcy stride into the room, his grey flannel breeches hanging halfway down his hips and his definitely not-ginger hair soaked through by the rain. *Oh my! He was Byronic!*

In a hurried manner he began an inquiry after her health, imputing his visit to a wish of hearing that she had been eating well. She replied, cordially, that she had enjoyed a hearty bowl of Frosties that very morning, and that he should have no worries on that account.

Darcy sat down for a few moments, and then getting up, walked about the room. Elizabeth was surprised, but said not a word. After a silence of several minutes, he came towards her in an agitated manner, and thus began:

'In vain have I struggled. It will not do. My feelings will not be repressed. You must allow me to tell you how ardently I wish to bind your limbs with cable ties and flog the living daylights out of you.'

Elizabeth's astonishment was beyond expression. She stared, coloured, doubted, and was silent. This he considered sufficient encouragement, and the list of every kinky thing he wanted to do to her, from tickling her fancy with feathers to sandpapering her nipples, immediately followed.

'You must understand, Elizabeth, that this will not be a boyfriend-girlfriend thing,' he concluded, running his hands through his copper locks in an agitated manner. 'I wish to formalize our relationship, and to that end, I have had my lawyer draw up a contract.'

Elizabeth struggled to compose herself. A marriage contract! This was the culmination of all her hopes. *Fitzwilliam Darcy was proposing!*

'Yes!' she breathed, her face alight with joy. 'I *shall* be your wife.'

Mr Darcy visibly blanched. 'My *wife*? I do not do *matrimony*, Elizabeth. I told you, my designs upon you are far darker than that. The document to which I refer is a kinky-sex contract. A detailed list of what I intend to do to you if you agree to be mine. A list which, if the reader of this book happens to be titillated by the BDSM scene, will no doubt be highly arousing. But to all other readers, will prove about as sexy as a list of borough council town-centre parking restrictions.'

From the pocket of his waistcoat he produced a slim roll of parchment, presenting it to Elizabeth with a curt nod of the head.

'Read!' he commanded.

With trembling fingers, Elizabeth unrolled the parchment.

> **This document, dated 28 February 1814 (hereafter known as 'the commencement date'), is a contract of voluntary sexual slavery between Mr Fitzwilliam Darcy ('the Dominant'), of Pemberley, Derbyshire, and Miss Elizabeth Bennet of Longbourn, Hertfordshire ('the Submissive').**

Oh my! What was this?

Mr Darcy, who was leaning against the mantelpiece with his eyes fixed upon her face, surveyed her hopefully. Elizabeth continued reading.

> The purpose of this contract is to allow the Submissive to explore her sensuality safely, with due respect for her needs and well-being. The Dominant and the Submissive agree and acknowledge that whatever occurs under the terms of this contract will be consensual and confidential, and subject to the agreed limits set out in this contract.

Mr Darcy fidgeted impatiently. 'Just skip to the dirty bits,' he urged. 'That's what everyone else does.'

Elizabeth unrolled the scroll further, and gave a gasp.

> Which of the following sexual acts are acceptable to the Submissive?
> 1. Slap and tickle
> 2. Rogering
> 3. Rutting
> 4. A bit of how's your father
> 5. Rumpy pumpy
> 6. Having clamps applied to your apple dumplings
> 7. Getting your nancy whacked with a cat o' nine tails ...

Her hands fell into her lap, and the document slithered to the floor.

'Say you'll sign, Elizabeth,' Darcy urged, his grey eyes smouldering. 'My penis depends upon it.'

'*Your penis depends upon it?*' Hot tears welled up in Elizabeth's eyes. 'Not your happiness, Mr Darcy? Have you no tender feelings at all?' Colour rose in her cheeks and her eyes flashed in anger. 'You cannot seriously expect me to accept these terms?'

'Am I to understand that you are *refusing* me?' Mr Darcy said incredulously, surprise etched upon his handsome features.

Elizabeth stood up, unsteadily, and declared in a voice that shook with emotion: 'You could not, Sir, have made me the offer of being your sex slave in any possible way that would have tempted me to accept it.'

Mr Darcy's astonishment was obvious, and he looked at her with an expression of mingled incredulity and mortification. She went on:

'From the very beginning, from the first moment, I may almost say, of my acquaintance with you, your manners impressed me with the fullest belief of your sex mania, your arrogance, and your verging-on-stalkerish behaviour. I have recognized you as an overgrown public schoolboy with a penis fixation. What is more, your constant exhortations to "Oooh, give it to me, baby," belong in a bad amateur porn film rather than a romantic novel. In short, Mr Darcy, your character needs more weight.'

Mr Darcy's mouth set in a grim line. 'I must take issue with you, Miss Bennet,' he remarked coldly. 'I am, as you know, unbelievably hot, which makes most of my character flaws forgivable. If a balding, paunchy middle-aged guy with bad shoes kept turning up when you least expected it, it would be creepy; when I do it, it is both ardent and deeply flattering.'

'You, Sir, are a badly drawn, one-dimensional figure!' Elizabeth countered. 'Fifty shades? More like two: "gagging for sex", that's one, and "in a bad mood".'

Anger made her voluble, and she continued: 'Who – *who* – I ask you, at twenty-seven, controls a multimillion global company just by occasionally picking up the phone and saying, "Talk to Peters", and "Get it there by Tuesday"? What do you actually *do* anyway? Furthermore, what heterosexual man even has tracks by Nelly Furtado on his iPod, let alone considers them a suitably erotic soundtrack for an S&M sex session?'

'Miss Bennet,' Mr Darcy remarked coldly, 'I do believe you are discussing the wrong book.'

Elizabeth checked herself. 'You are correct, Mr Darcy,' she replied gravely. 'On that point I must beg your forgiveness. It is somewhat confusing being in a mash-up of two very different novels.'

'No matter, Miss Bennet,' Darcy answered curtly. 'I believe you have made your intentions clear. I perfectly comprehend your feelings. Forgive me for prevailing upon your time, and accept my best wishes for your health and happiness.'

And with these words he hastily left the room, his grey flannel breeches hanging so far off his hips that Elizabeth was afforded a last, tantalizing glimpse of his bicycle rack, and she heard him the next moment open the front door and quit the house.

The tumult of Elizabeth's mind was now painfully great. Her astonishment, as she reflected upon what had passed, was increased by every review of it. That Mr Darcy should suggest that she become his sex slave! It was an abomination! And yet, the tumult of Elizabeth's ladyparts was equally great. Why did her heart race, and her bloomers quiver, at the thought of submitting to Mr Darcy's every whim? She picked up the contract again, and glanced at the licentious, shocking words written therein.

'Bondage with curtain trimmings,' she read. 'Blindfolding'; 'gagging'; 'spreader bars' – what could they possibly be? Heat suffused her body, and she fanned herself frantically with the parchment. To think that she, Elizabeth Bennet, was tempted to abandon her family and her reputation, and enter a world of sado-masochistic sex! And that Fitzwilliam Darcy should be her Master, to deal with her as he pleased!

'You're not seriously considering it?' her Subconscious

asked incredulously. 'He's clearly unstable.'

Elizabeth sighed. 'But leaving aside his constant innuendo and smutty talk, and his controlling personality, and his arrogance, and jealousy, and slightly camp dress sense and *appalling* taste in music, I think he's basically a nice guy. What do *you* think, Inner Slapper?'

At that moment, her Inner Slapper burst out of her metaphorical closet wearing a peephole basque and crotchless knickers. 'Ta-da!' she trilled. 'Now, which way do I go for the seeing-to?'

Elizabeth awoke the next morning to the same thoughts and meditations which had at length closed her eyes. It was impossible to think of anything else but Mr Darcy's kinky proposal, and she resolved, soon after breakfast, to read the contract in more detail. Taking the parchment out of a drawer, in which she had concealed it the evening before, she unrolled it fully and laid it upon her bureau.

She read with an eagerness which hardly left her power of comprehension. Indeed, many of the terms in the document were beyond her understanding:

* The Dominant may use the Submissive in any sexual way he sees fit, at any time, except when the vicar comes for tea.
* The Dominant may flog, spank, whip or corporally punish the Submissive for his own personal gratification.
* The Submissive shall accept the Dominant as her master, and obey all the rules set out in this agreement.
* The Submissive shall not touch the Dominant at any time.

✳ The Dominant and the Submissive will make
 use of safe words which will be used to bring events to
 a close.

✳ In addition, the Submissive will ensure she
 achieves eight hours' sleep at night, eats from a list
 of foods provided by the Dominant, and keeps herself
 waxed and exfoliated at all times.

Waxed? Exfoliated? Elizabeth had never heard those terms before, but they sounded distinctly uncomfortable. But then this whole scheme was madness! That she should submit to the whims of a debauched rakehell such as Mr Darcy, allow him to use her ill and then, no doubt, cast her aside ... And yet, there was something in his offer that tempted her.

Taking up her quill, and a sheet of hotpressed paper from her bureau, she hastily wrote:

Dear Mr Darcy,
Regarding our discussion of yesterday, I find myself both shocked and offended by your offer of sexual slavery. However, contrary to all good sense, I am curious to know more about the lifestyle you are proposing. Having perused the document more closely at my leisure, I have a number of questions. Chiefly, what is exfoliation?
Yours, Elizabeth Bennet

'I shall send this at once,' she decided. 'Where is Lapptop?' A ring of the bell duly summoned the aged manservant, and Elizabeth instructed him to hasten to Rosings Park and deliver the note personally to Mr Darcy. She had to wait less than an hour for his reply:

My dear Miss Bennet,
Exfoliation is the topical application of an unguent, of an abrasive nature, in order to smooth and beautify the skin. This you may do using a cosmetic formulation. However, I would rather you allow me to exfoliate you all over using my chin stubble.
Yours, Fitzwilliam Darcy

All over? Elizabeth felt a pull deep in her belly. She took another sheet of writing paper from her bureau, and penned:

Mr Darcy,
What, pray, are safe words?
Yours, Elizabeth Bennet
PS No fisting of any kind.

After luncheon, Darcy's reply was brought back by a weary Lapptop.

Miss Bennet,
If, at any time during our kinky sex-play, you utter the words 'fluffy kittens' or 'I wuv you!', I shall immediately lose tumescence and, as such, our encounter will be over. I trust this sets your mind at rest.
Yours, etc.

Dear Mr Darcy,
Why may I not touch you? Is your member, perchance, the size of a button mushroom?'
Elizabeth Bennet

Dear Miss Bennet,
You ask too many questions. Impertinent young ladies are liable to receive chastisement. The next time I see you in the grounds of Rosings, I shall have to remove your undergarments and thrash you with my riding crop.'
Yours, Fitzwilliam Darcy

Dear Mr Darcy,
You may have difficulty in removing my under-garments, as next time I have occasion to meet you, I do not intend to wear any.
Elizabeth

Dear Miss Bennet,
Is it your intention to inflame me? Then you must be prepared for the consequences.
F.

By now Lapptop was wheezing and on the verge of collapse, and Elizabeth, concerned for the elderly servant's wellbeing, decided it was in his best interests not to reply. She spent the remainder of the evening playing whist with Charlotte, and had just excused herself and gone up to her bedchamber when there was a tap upon the door. It was Charlotte, with a note for Elizabeth.

'Forgive me for disturbing you, Lizzy, but this just arrived from Rosings. Mrs Blackberry brought it over.'

So Mr Darcy now had Lady Catherine's staff delivering messages! 'Thank you, Charlotte,' said she. 'I will attend to it in the morning.'

Charlotte hesitated. 'Mrs Blackberry is still downstairs, awaiting your reply.'

'Oh, Charlotte, I am far too tired to write any more this

evening. Please be so good as to tell her to go back.'

Charlotte retreated, and Elizabeth, unable to contain her curiosity, opened the letter with eager fingers.

> *Miss Bennet,*
> You have not replied. I do not like to be kept waiting. I shall be forced to call in at Hunsford Parsonage drag you out to my carriage and xxxxx your xxxx with my xxxxx. And when you're begging for mercy, I shall xxxx xxxxx your xxxx until you xxxxxxx.
> Yours, etc.

How frustrating! Raindrops had smudged some of Mr Darcy's words. She could only guess at his intentions. She would, she determined, sleep on the matter, and consider it afresh the next day. She had not realized how much the tumult of her emotions had exhausted her, and it took only moments for her to fall into an uneasy slumber.

She was dreaming of fluffy kittens wearing nipple clamps when something started her out of sleep. The fire was dwindling in the grate, its embers sending out an eerie glow. In the half-light, Elizabeth discerned a shape, looming menacingly in the corner of the room by the window. *Oh my! There was someone in her bedchamber!*

Fitzwilliam Darcy stepped out of the shadows.

'Why did you not reply to my note, Miss Bennet?' he asked huskily.

'My goodness! Mr Darcy! How are you here, at Hunsford?' Elizabeth clutched the counterpane tightly; her heart was pounding and her breath came in shallow gasps. *What the holy hell was he doing in her room?*

'Oh, I came in the carriage,' he said in a low murmur, his eyes burning with intensity. 'And then I got out, cleaned myself up and walked over here.'

He ran his hands repeatedly through his copper locks, an anguished look upon his face. 'Scabies,' he explained.

Suddenly, he flung himself towards the bed and gripped Elizabeth by the shoulders. 'When I did not hear from you, I knew I *had* to see you. I cannot stop thinking about you, Miss Bennet. You. Are. So. Sweet.' His grey eyes were like pile drivers, hammering shards of intensity into her soul. Briefly, a look of uncertainty flashed across his face. 'Am I being passionate, or is this a bit creepy?' he asked in a low voice.

Elizabeth pondered the question. 'Many young ladies would undoubtedly call the night watchmen,' she conceded. 'But having no previous experience of courtship, I find myself flattered by your attentions.'

Mr Darcy seemed to relax. Cupping her chin in one hand, and her breast in the other, he said softly, 'Promise me, Elizabeth, that you will consider the terms of the contract. It would mean everything to me to have you as my kinky-sex slave.'

Elizabeth could feel her resistance melting away. 'Fitzwilliam ...' she breathed, lifting her face to his, longing to feel his lips upon hers.

'Urrrgh, yucky!' Mr Darcy cried, starting back in horror. 'No kissing!'

Elizabeth's blue eyes pricked with tears. 'You never kiss?'

'Bleurgh! No way. It's soppy.'

Elizabeth was crestfallen. It was as she had first thought. Fitzwilliam Darcy had no tender feelings. He was nothing but a machine. A sex machine. Get up, get on up. Get up, get on up, stay on the scene, like a ...

'Elizabeth, are you unwell?' Mr Darcy was staring at her intensely, his brow furrowed with concern.

'I'm sorry?'

'You were singing,' he explained.

Elizabeth shook herself. 'Oh, forgive me, I got carried away.' She gazed up into his grey eyes: they seemed cold, fathomless – perhaps, after all, he was beyond her reach?

Perhaps he could not be saved?

'I am leaving Hunsford in a matter of days,' she said firmly. 'I think it best if we do not see each other again until then. I shall consider your offer while I am at Longbourn and send word to you.'

Mr Darcy looked pained.

'I have hurt your feelings,' Elizabeth said gently.

'No. Well, yes, but I've got terrible indigestion today. Too many pickled eggs.'

He stood up abruptly. 'If that is what you wish, Miss Bennet,' he said coolly. 'I shall not trouble you further. Unless you have any Gaviscon?'

Elizabeth shook her head, tears beginning to spill over her dark lashes. Mr Darcy leapt out of the window with one athletic bound, and a second later she heard a crunch and a muffled, 'Bloody hell!' as he landed in a rose bush below. Burying her face in her pillow, she let her tears flow. He was gone – the only man she had ever desired. The only man she had ever loved. Gone, gone with the wind.

Elizabeth's absence from Longbourn had long been mourned by Jane, and upon the former's return, the two sisters greeted each other with much cordiality. Elizabeth's impatience to acquaint Jane with all that had occurred could not be overcome, and as soon as she was able, she related to her the chief of the encounters between Mr Darcy and herself.

'Are you at all tempted by his offer, Lizzy?' Jane asked.

Elizabeth coloured. 'I confess I am, just a little,' she replied in a hushed voice.

Jane pondered for a moment. 'I suppose I can see why. I imagine Mr Darcy would be most appealing as a lover, if his size fourteen feet are anything to go by.'

'And what of Mr Bingley?' Elizabeth asked. 'Is he as much in love with you as ever?'

Jane sighed. 'I have heard nothing, Lizzy. He has not written to me at all, nor has he visited.'

Her sister's surprising news tainted Elizabeth's own joy at her return. Mrs Bennet, however, was determined to celebrate Elizabeth's homecoming and to spread word about the neighbourhood of her daughter's imminent deflowering. 'My Lizzy! A sex slave!' she exclaimed in delight. 'Who would have thought it! I can hold my head up in society at last. And with Lydia now a firm favourite among the officers, she is sure to be rogered before Easter!'

Day after day passed without bringing any word of Bingley other than the news, which prevailed in Meryton, that he intended not to spend Easter at Netherfield, but to go surfing in Maui instead. Unwilling as Elizabeth was to admit the inconstancy of Mr Bingley, and all that might imply about his close friend Mr Darcy's own character, she could not help but believe that the attractions of South Sea island beauties clad in string micro-bikinis could only weaken his attachment to her sister.

At last a letter arrived that brought an end to uncertainty. With trembling fingers, Jane tore open the seal and read in silence.

My dear Jane,
I do so hope you are well. Just to let you know, I will be out of the country for a while. I'm going to the Pacific to catch some waves. Apparently, it's a

big, big ocean on the whole other side of the world!
And there was me thinking the rest of the world was
made of cheese! Or is that the moon? Oh well,
L8ers babe,
E x

Hope was over, entirely over, and Jane could find
nothing in Bingley's missive to give her any comfort.
Elizabeth, to whom Jane very soon communicated the
contents of the letter, heard it all in silent indignation.
The curly haired fuckstick! Her heart was divided between
concern for her sister, and resentment towards Mr Bingley.
That he was truly fond of Jane, she doubted no more than
she had ever done, and much as she had always been
disposed to like him, she could not think without anger
that he was prepared to sacrifice his own chance of marital
happiness to the caprice of a pathetic adolescent desire to
go backpacking.

'Whatever did you do to drive him away, you silly girl?'
chided Mrs Bennet. 'Or, more importantly, what did you
not do? Lord, do not tell me you introduced a "no touching
beneath the bodice" rule?'

'Please desist, Mother!' complained Jane. 'You have no
idea of the pain you give me with your continual reflections
on Mr Bingley. Let us leave the matter,' she continued sadly.
'He will soon be forgot, and we shall be as we were before.'

Elizabeth looked at her sister with incredulity.

'Dear Jane, you are too good! I wish I had half your
sweetness of temper. He is a commitment-phobic twat,
and if I ever see him again, I shall certainly tell him so.'

'Oh Lizzy, I beg you not to!'

'No, how dare he lead you to believe his attachment to
you was genuine, if he was intending all the time to bugger
off to Hawaii?'

Jane smiled sadly. 'Please, Lizzy, you have nothing to reproach him with. If there was a misunderstanding, I assure you, it was all on my part. Pray, let us not speak of him again.'

Elizabeth could not oppose such a wish, and from that point on, Mr Bingley's name was scarcely mentioned by either of them. Mrs Bennet, however, still mourned Mr Bingley's leaving Netherfield, and was convinced that he would return after his Pacific-island sojourn, and if Jane would only put out this time, she might engage his interest once more.

One morning after breakfast, when Elizabeth was returning to Longbourn from a stroll about the grounds, she encountered a bedraggled-looking young woman waiting on the steps at the front of the house. On seeing Elizabeth, the woman bobbed into a curtsey, and announced, 'I've bought a note, if it please you, Miss. From Mr Darcy of Pemberley.'

The young woman was pale and seemed exhausted; her boots and the hem of her gown were splattered with mud.

'Heavens, have you come all the way from Derbyshire?' Elizabeth asked in surprise.

'Mr Darcy told me it was urgent, Miss, and not to rest until I had put the note into your very own hands. I've been walking for four days solid.' With that, she took from her pocket a piece of paper, folded and sealed with the distinctive Darcy coat of arms: two cocks rampant.

Elizabeth murmured her thanks, and tore open the seal. She read:

Dear Miss Bennet,
I could not wait any longer for correspondence from you, so I have taken the liberty of sending a female, in order that the conversation we began at Hunsford might be brought to a satisfactory conclusion.

'I still do not understand why Mr Darcy thought it fit to send you,' Elizabeth remarked, addressing the servant. 'It is mystifying. You must have been vulnerable to all manner of dangers upon the road.'

'Mr Darcy said he wouldn't have trusted a young man to deliver the note, Miss. Females are more reliable, he said.'

There *had* to be a more efficient and speedy means of communication than this, Elizabeth thought. Maybe one day, far in the future, someone would devise another method. Until then, she supposed, females would have to suffice.

She read on:

Now that you have had time to ruminate, I hope that you find yourself more amenable to considering the terms of my sex contract. Believe me, Elizabeth, I want nothing more than for you to become my Submissive. I believe you would attain pleasure from it, too. Please agree to an imminent meeting, to discuss the hard and soft limits, and any queries or concerns you may have. Send your reply by means of another female. I will be waiting.
Yours, Fitzwilliam Darcy

Elizabeth felt light-headed; her mouth was suddenly uncomfortably dry. She had, in truth, hoped that Mr Darcy would somehow forget the matter of the contract. But it was evident that if she wished for any sort of relationship with this complicated, brooding billionaire, it would have to be on formal terms.

Memories of Mr Darcy slapping her reticule came, unbidden, into her head. The humiliation of that moment! And yet, although she had been shaken, she had to admit she had also been stirred. He was so masterful, so in control, that it was easy to imagine herself surrendering to his whims – allowing herself to be strapped up, stripped naked, and left vulnerable, for Mr Darcy to do with as he pleased … The thought was arousing, and she let out a low moan.

'Are you all right, Miss?'

The servant's gratingly common accent brought Elizabeth back to reality with a jolt.

'Thank you,' she replied, fanning herself with the letter. 'Go round the back way into the kitchens and take some refreshment. No doubt you are tired.'

'But the reply, Miss?'

'Do not trouble yourself. I shall send a female of my own in due course.'

In fact, Elizabeth retired to her room as soon as she had taken off her coat and bonnet, in order to pen a letter to Mr Darcy. With trembling fingers, she dipped her quill in ink and wrote:

Mr Darcy,
Your missive reached me at a time of great inner turmoil. I have been betwixt and between, I have blown hot and cold, I have hemmed and hawed – I particularly enjoyed the hawing – but still I am no closer to making a decision.

Once again, you have the advantage of me, Sir.

As you well know, I am largely ignorant of the ways of the flesh. My sisters are as ill-informed as I, and I dare not ask Mama for fear of having her tell me yet again, and in great detail, about the time she gave the Prince Regent a blow job. I have considered consulting Old Granny Google in the village, who in her youth was mistress to several gentlemen of quality and knows much of these matters. Although I am not sure how much she can tell me of sado-masochism. From the stories she tells the dairymaids, I don't think it was particularly her scene.

But my questions about sexual matters can wait. The matter that perplexes me most is why you demeaned yourself at Rosings, by wearing those tiny leather hotpants? What hold does Lady Catherine have over you? And if I were to allow you to become my Dominant, would I be required to don similar attire?

Yours, Elizabeth Bennet

She waited until the afternoon, and then sent one of the footmen into Meryton with instructions to find a suitably robust young woman capable of delivering the message to Derbyshire. Within days, another female arrived at Longbourn, sent by Mr Darcy.

My dear Miss Bennet,
Lady Catherine has no hold over me – I serve her willingly. She was my Dominant for many years after I left Beaton, and she taught me everything I know about sexual congress. As for the hotpants, if you wish not to wear them, I shall not force the issue. However, I would very much enjoy the sight

of leather cutting into your ripe young buttocks.

As for your questions about the sexual act, pray address them to me. I will endeavour to answer them honestly.

Yours, etc., Fitzwilliam

Another willing female was dispatched from Longbourn, with Elizabeth's note:

Mr Darcy,
Lady Catherine was your Dominant? But she is so hideously old – at least thirty-five! And you yourself must have been young and vulnerable. How could she do it?

Elizabeth Bennet
PS Can you get with child just by kissing?

Miss Bennet,
Lady Catherine saved me from myself. If it wasn't for her I would be a fucked-up, humourless, control-freak loser. As opposed to a fucked-up, humourless, control-freak successful billionaire.

In answer to your question, no. You get with child by having a 'special cuddle'. And rest assured, we shan't be having many of those.

Yours, etc.

Mr Darcy,
Is it true that if a man's member has risen, it is bad for his health if he is subsequently unable to achieve release?

Yours, Elizabeth

Miss Bennet,
Yes. He might die. We must make sure this *never happens.*
Fitzwilliam

Females were sent to and fro between them for the next fortnight, until Mr Darcy wrote to inform her that he would shortly be calling in at Netherfield at the request of Mr Bingley, in order to take care of some estate business on his behalf. The news threw Elizabeth into turmoil. Although her Inner Slapper yearned to see Mr Darcy again – to smell his musky body wash, and to be probed by his piercing grey eyes – her Subconscious told her to beware. With every moment spent with Mr Darcy, she edged nearer to the precipice, the precipice that loomed over a great chasm of disrepute and perversion. Would she plunge over? Hmm, I can't imagine.

At seven the next evening, Taylor arrived at Longbourn in a small phaeton drawn by a grey mare.

'I'm to collect you, Miss, and take you to the Roger Inn.' His plebeian face wore an apologetic expression. 'Mr Darcy's orders, Miss.'

Mr Darcy's orders indeed! Elizabeth's hackles rose. He was so arrogant! And yet so irresistibly horny!

'Thank you, Taylor. I will be just a moment.'

Seizing a cape, and grabbing her reticule in a most unladylike fashion, Elizabeth quit the house. She was aware of Mrs Bennet looking out at her through her bedroom window. *What* is *Mama trying to tell me?* she wondered, watching her mother alternately pointing down at her, and then frantically pushing her bosom up and down with both hands so that it quivered like a giant blancmange.

Taylor helped Elizabeth into the phaeton. The air was chilly, and she pulled her cape tightly round herself as they set off on the short journey to Meryton.

'Is Mr Darcy well?' she called up to Taylor.

'As well as can be expected, Miss,' came the gruff reply.

'Oh, has he been ill?'

Taylor continued to stare straight ahead. 'He has been ... distracted, Miss. Not his usual self.'

For one moment, Elizabeth allowed herself to think that *she* might be the reason for Mr Darcy's preoccupation. 'I confess, I am not altogether familiar with Mr Darcy's usual self,' she remarked. 'How would you rate his general character, Taylor? Does he treat his servants well?'

Taylor turned and smiled, and his stubbly lower-class face looked almost human. 'In that regard he's the best that ever was, Miss. We all get a shilling a year, and one-and-a-half days' holiday.'

'A generous arrangement indeed!'

'Oh, but Mr Darcy is a wonderful man,' Taylor continued. 'All the good works he does with the poor! And there's no denying he cherishes his little sister. There is nothing he would not do for her.'

This must have been the Georgiana that Elizabeth had heard so much about from Carrotslime and Looseata – the young lady they felt would make a more suitable match for Bingley than her own dear sister Jane.

'So, we have established that he is a loving brother, and a beneficent employer. He must have *some* faults, surely?' she said teasingly.

'Well, Miss, now you come to mention it, he *is* an incurable sex maniac.'

They trotted on in silence, and on rounding the curve of the road leading up to the inn, Elizabeth could feel her stomach fluttering in anticipation. *Holy crap, she was nervous.*

Mr Darcy was standing outside the inn, leaning

casually against a low wall, drinking a glass of claret. He was dressed in his customary attire: white linen shirt, grey breeches and, this time, just to ring the changes, a sombrero. Beneath it, his hair was sexily tousled. She had forgotten how *freakin' hot* he was! Elizabeth stared slack-jawed for a few moments.

'Allow me, Miss Bennet.' Mr Darcy stepped forward to wipe the drool from Elizabeth's chin. With one sexy hand he lifted her down from the phaeton. Cocking his head to one side, and his leg to the other side, Mr Darcy surveyed her.

'You look beautiful, Elizabeth,' he murmured appreciatively. 'Your gown becomes you.'

Elizabeth smiled shyly. See-through lace had been the right choice after all.

'Shall we go in?'

Together they traversed the snug bar, where gnarly handed farmers and rough-looking labourers were hunched over their flagons of cheap ale, and entered a private dining room to the left. Elizabeth gave a gasp: the table was laden with baskets of cut flowers and piles of fresh and sugared fruits. In the chandelier above, three score candles glowed seductively, their light glinting off the silver cutlery and crystal glassware below. It was romantic beyond her wildest dreams. Mr Darcy pulled out a chair for her at one end of the long trestle table, then took his place at the other end, directly opposite her. He smiled, and his long fingers reached out to pluck a cherry from a nearby plate.

'You have thought about my contract, Miss Bennet?' His voice was ardent, and his eyes burned into hers like sexy blowtorches.

Elizabeth took a sip of her wine.

'I have, Mr Darcy,' she declared. 'But I cannot agree to

everything you ask.'

'Pardon?'

'I said, *I cannot agree to everything you ask*. Should we sit a little closer, do you think?'

'It will be fine,' Mr Darcy shouted, 'as long as we both annunciate.'

Reaching into his waistcoat pocket, he pulled out a sheaf of papers. 'I have a copy of the contract here.'

Elizabeth took another nervous gulp of wine. Mr Darcy looked down and scanned the first page.

'Let me see… *No fisting*'. A serving maid who had just entered the room with a jug of ale gave a start, splashing froth all over the floor. 'I think we have established that already,' Mr Darcy continued. 'Do you have any other concerns, Elizabeth?'

'I do not know where to begin,' Elizabeth said, exasperated. 'What you ask of me is beyond my experience.'

'Then let us go over the contract point by point,' Mr Darcy replied, laying out the papers in front of him on the table.

'Item 1: Social activities,' Mr Darcy began. 'The Dominant is free to visit the gaming tables, any house of ill repute, or his drinking club, whenever he so chooses. When the Submissive asks where he is going, he is entitled to say, "Just out." The Submissive may leave the premises once every two months, in the company of Taylor, in order to purchase new sexy underthings.'

Darcy paused. 'There is no negotiation on those particular points, Elizabeth,' he said firmly. 'You are not safe walking about on your own. I need to keep you from harm.'

'Item 2: Personal grooming. The Submissive shall keep herself waxed, shaved, exfoliated, plucked, bleached and deodorized at all times.'

Oh my! Elizabeth blushed furiously as Mr Darcy fixed her with his smouldering grey eyes. 'I want you like an oven-ready chicken, Elizabeth,' he said seductively, 'ready for basting. Agreed?'

Elizabeth nodded. The two sips of wine she had taken were making her head swim, and she was finding it hard to focus.

'Item 3: Food. The Submissive shall eat when the Dominant gives the command. She may not choose her own meals, but will eat from a menu compiled by the Dominant and prepared by the housekeeper, Mrs Jones. Foods that will not directly benefit the Submissive's health, such as chocolate, are prohibited.'

'Hang on, *no chocolate*?' Elizabeth asked, finding her voice at last. 'That is most definitely a deal breaker for me, Mr Darcy.'

Mr Darcy glowered. For a few moments he was quiet, surveying her with eyes that shone like shiny things. Elizabeth sensed that the author was running out of ways to describe his eyes. 'Very well,' he said at last. 'Chocolate will be permitted.'

Elizabeth smiled. It was a small victory, she knew, but what was a life of sexual slavery without chocolate?

'Item 4: Exercise. The Submissive shall not jog, run, play contact sports, swim, ride or undertake any other activity that might put her at risk of injury. She may, however, indulge in yoga or gentle aerobics, provided she wears only a tiny Lycra thong and the Dominant is allowed to watch.'

'Are country walks permitted?' asked Elizabeth, thinking how much she would miss her daily outings were they to be outlawed.

'I have told you, Miss Bennet, I do not want you wandering about on your own. You might trip over a tussock.'

'Perhaps if Taylor were to accompany me?'

Mr Darcy's eyes narrowed as he considered the request. 'I cannot consent to this,' he said finally. 'The countryside surrounding Pemberley is hilly, and I will permit perambulation only where the gradient of the land is 1:1. Shall we continue?'

'Item 5: Domestic duties. The Submissive shall be responsible for the washing, ironing and dusting, and shall clean the bathroom twice a week. If the Dominant happens to drop his socks and pants on the floor, the Submissive shall pick them up and put them in the laundry basket. If the Dominant on occasion leaves the toilet seat up, the Submissive shall put it down ...'

'Hang on a minute, there's something really dodgy about this,' muttered Elizabeth's Subconscious.

'...The Submissive has the right to ask the Dominant to put out the bins once a week, and to mend any wonky shelves that may require re-aligning. Although whether or not he complies is the Dominant's prerogative.'

Just then, Mr Darcy was interrupted by the arrival of another serving maid, bringing the first course. She set down a dish of braised ox tongue on the table, and Mr Darcy prodded it gently with his fork. 'I hope you enjoy tongue, Miss Bennet,' he said teasingly.

Elizabeth sighed and raised her eyebrows. 'Are you making an oblique reference to cunnilingus, Mr Darcy?'

Mr Darcy gave a start. For a moment he struggled to speak, and could only stare at her in confusion. 'We both know that's not how this works,' he spluttered at last. '*I* make the innuendos, and you just blush.'

'Oh. Forgive me, I don't know what came over me,' said Elizabeth apologetically. A blush crept prettily across her flawless cheeks. 'No, Mr Darcy,' she said in a shocked whisper. 'I am unused to tongue.'

'You will have to develop a taste for it if you are to reside at Pemberley with me,' Mr Darcy said lasciviously, his grey eyes raking her body.

To reside with him at Pemberley! Elizabeth's heart beat a little faster.

Mr Darcy poured gravy over his tongue and sprinkled it liberally with pepper.

'You have barely touched your food, Elizabeth,' he said curtly. 'You must eat. You will need the same calorific intake as an Olympic rower if you are to keep up with my intensive boffing regime. It will be the equivalent of competing in the Oxford-Cambridge boat race every single day.'

Elizabeth fanned herself with her napkin. 'Will it truly be that arduous, Mr Darcy?'

'Oh, indeed it will, Miss Bennet,' Mr Darcy said in a low voice, his grey eyes like molten steel. 'When I have it off, I have it off *hard*.'

Elizabeth winced. Mr Darcy took another mouthful of tongue.

'Now that we are in agreement on the basic rules, what do you say? Will you come to Pemberley with me, and be my sex slave?'

Elizabeth, deep in thought, bit her nails. Mr Darcy gave a growl of desire.

'Say yes, Elizabeth.'

She gazed into his smoky-grey eyes, which were sizzling now, like sausages on a griddle. 'Yes,' she breathed.

'Then let's not wait Elizabeth,' he murmured back. 'Right now all I can think of is ripping off your dress and thwacking you until you are black and blue.'

Elizabeth's nerves began to tingle. His voice was irresistible, and rivulets of desire cascaded over her whole body.

'I want you, Elizabeth. Here. Now.'

Elizabeth glanced anxiously at the two servants who were hovering by the door.

'And I know that you want me too.'

She frowned. His arrogance knew no bounds!

'How can you be so certain?' she enquired.

'I know because your body gives you away,' Mr Darcy said confidently. 'You are flushed, your breathing has changed, and you have just stripped off and are lying naked on the table with only a few frosted grapes covering your modesty.'

Elizabeth glanced down. *Holy heck, he was right!* She hadn't even realized that she'd been disrobing. Why did he have such a powerful effect upon her?

'Taylor!' At Mr Darcy's command, Taylor's stubbled face appeared from beneath the tablecloth.

'Be so good as to preserve Miss Bennet's modesty.' Averting his eyes, Taylor laid his cloak gently across Elizabeth's body.

'I have taken the liberty of booking a room,' Mr Darcy said. 'Taylor will carry you up there.'

'Are you coming too?' Elizabeth enquired, as Taylor scooped her into his lower-class arms. The wine she had drunk was making her head swim, but also making her bold.

'I have never slept in the same room as a woman, Elizabeth,' Mr Darcy said darkly, and for a moment his beautiful face took on a mournful expression.

'Then perhaps you will make an exception tonight?'

'I cannot sleep beside you,' he said sadly. 'But I will come up later for a grope.'

A grope! Her insides turned to liquid at his words.

Carefully, Taylor carried Elizabeth through a small door in the corner of the room which led to a narrow staircase.

Thank heavens she did not have to go through the public bar, Elizabeth thought gratefully, and be exposed to the ogles of the lower classes. The stairs wound up to a tiny attic room, sparsely decorated but for a bed and a washstand.

'Thank you, Taylor,' Elizabeth said as the burly manservant set her down gently upon the floorboards. Taylor nodded briefly and turned to go, then seemed to hesitate.

'Just one thing, Miss,' he said hurriedly, thrusting something into her hands. 'You might need this.'

He had vanished before Elizabeth had had a chance to read the label on the tiny tube he had given her. 'Hmm, KY Jelly,' she said aloud. 'Sounds delicious. Maybe it's for toast?' She rubbed a little on her lips and immediately pulled a face. She was sorry to scorn Taylor's gift, but it was nowhere near as good as Cragg's marmalade.

Flinging the jelly onto the washstand, Elizabeth threw herself upon the bed and wrapped the coverlet about herself. Mr Darcy would be here soon; she had to stay awake. Yet the two sips of wine she had partaken of, and her fraught nerves, meant that sleep was soon upon her. At one point, she was vaguely aware of Mr Darcy slipping naked into her bed – or did she dream it all? He reached out a hand, cupped her right breast and squeezed it gently.

'Honk! Honk!' he whispered.

If ever a man needed saving from himself, Elizabeth thought through the fog of sleep, it was Fitzwiliam Darcy.

It seemed to Elizabeth that she had barely closed her eyes at all when the sun began creeping in at the window, like a burglar with nice warm hands. Sighing, she nestled deeper in the bedsheets, enjoying the feel of cotton against her naked body. Today she was leaving Hertfordshire. Could she really give up her life at Longbourn, her turns about the parlour and her needlepoint, her pianoforte and her plans for replanting the herb garden, for the life of a sexual submissive?

The window was ajar, and Elizabeth could hear voices in the yard below. Above the usual chatter of serving maids and stablehands, she recognized Taylor's gruff tones, and Mr Darcy's deep, sexy ones. Her curiosity roused, she threw off the bedcovers and pulled back the curtain. *Holy inflatable rubber sphere!* There, in the inn forecourt, was a magnificent sight – Charlie Tango, standing proud and ready, swollen to full size, waiting for her. She had never seen anything so breathtakingly enormous. Mr Darcy, clad in an open-necked white shirt and tight grey flannel riding breeches, did not look up, so engrossed was he in humping sandbags over the rim of Charlie Tango's basket.

Elizabeth stood for a moment, transfixed by the scene below. By now, dawn was sending out fingers of light, which gently tickled the distant hills and excitedly probed the furrowed fields. Sunlight sprinkled down on Mr Darcy's lithe, athletic form like golden showers, causing his copper highlights to glow bright ginger. Elizabeth drank in the sight of him. Once again, she felt the familiar tug of desire for this sexy, complicated billionaire landowner.

Hurriedly, she dressed in the flimsy gown she had been wearing the night before. At the very moment she was about the quit the room, she happened to spy a pair of men's longjohns draped over a chair beside her bed. So it was no dream – Mr Darcy had been in her room after all.

Elizabeth smiled to herself. Dare she? Hurriedly, she slipped the longjohns on over her bestockinged legs. Mr Darcy would never guess she was wearing his undergarments! Although he might suspect something amiss if she had to keep on clawing at her nether regions, she thought to herself as she scratched vigorously at her ladyparts; the worsted really was uncomfortably itchy.

Still rubbing most indecorously, Elizabeth ran from her room and down the staircase, through the bar and out into the yard. Despite her reservations about leaving Hertfordshire, she could feel only giddy excitement when looking at Charlie Tango close up. Everything about the balloon was impressive, from its yellow and red striped canopy, to the capacious wicker basket beneath.

Mr Darcy's face was impassive. 'Good morning, Miss Bennet,' he said coolly. 'We will be departing shortly. If you search in my breeches pocket, you will find a buttered scone that I have prepared for your breakfast.'

'I am not hu...' Elizabeth began, but the look on Mr Darcy's face warned her not to deny his request. He was, after all, her Master now.

'Eat, Elizabeth,' he entreated. 'Do this one thing for me.' His grey eyes looked suddenly sad, like two koalas whose eucalyptus grove had been cut down by property developers.

Elizabeth was moved. 'Very well. I shall partake of breakfast this once, if it pleases you,' she declared. Stepping forward, she slipped her hand into Mr Darcy's front pocket – no mean feat, for his breeches were exceptionally close fitting. Several minutes of searching produced no results, and Elizabeth withdrew her hand with a puzzled look upon her face.

'Try the other pocket,' Mr Darcy suggested.

Elizabeth's fingers dug deep, probing into every crevice, but once again her search proved fruitless. Mr Darcy appeared agitated; his eyes had taken on a wild look, and his breathing was becoming more rapid. Losing a scone was apparently causing him a great deal of distress.

'It is not there!' Elizabeth said, exasperated by her quest for a breakfast she did not even want.

'Keep looking!' Mr Darcy gasped. 'I know it's there somewhere!'

At once, Elizabeth realized Mr Darcy's true motivation. 'There is no scone, is there, Mr Darcy?' she accused him, withdrawing her hand from his pocket at once. 'I cannot believe you are attempting to gain sexual pleasure at my expense, in my innocent search for a buttered scone.'

Mr Darcy's eyes locked on to hers, and what she saw there almost made Elizabeth swoon. 'Can you blame me, Miss Bennet?' he said huskily. 'I've told you, I find it hard to control myself with you.' He sighed deeply. 'Forgive me, I have a dark, dark heart.'

These were not the words of Fitzwilliam Darcy the sex-pervert billionaire, Elizabeth realized; this was Fitzwilliam Darcy the damaged schoolboy speaking. If only he would display his vulnerable parts to me more often, Elizabeth thought ruefully. She would give anything to see them.

Suddenly, Mr Darcy's mood seemed to switch, and his manner became formal once again.

'Let us get you into the basket, Miss Bennet,' he said, leaning down and lifting up Elizabeth in his hunky arms. He. Was. So. Strong. She was as helpless as a rag doll, his to do with as he pleased. To play dolly tea parties, or, more likely, to boff senseless. The power was in his hands.

Like he was fondling a particularly fine piece of bone china, Mr Darcy gently set her down inside the basket, all the while never taking his sexy eyes off hers. He picked up his own tailcoat and wrapped it tightly about her shoulders.

'We need to strap you in, Miss Bennet,' he murmured. 'We all know how accident-prone you are.' There were myriad buckles and fastenings attached to the basket's sides, and Mr Darcy set about pinioning Elizabeth to a bench seat. His breathing became faster as he snapped and tightened each leather strap, and Elizabeth feared he would excite his sensibilities once more, and she would have another scone situation on her hands. But finally, after tying strands of her hair to the balloon cables, Mr Darcy seemed satisfied, and stepped back to admire his handiwork.

'Are you ready, Miss Bennet?' he breathed. She nodded, her nerves tingling with excitement. 'Then here we go, baby!' he exclaimed. And with that, he let out a blast of gas.

Elizabeth gasped in delight as Charlie Tango began, slowly, to rise from its moorings. More blasts of gas, and the balloon rose higher still, up past the elm trees that lined the road to the inn, up until all she could hear was the rush of the wind, and Taylor was but a stubbly visaged speck upon the ground.

At first, Elizabeth gripped the edge of the basket so tightly her fingers ached, but as they ascended, she gradually released her hold. Mr Darcy made her feel safe. He was so capable, so in command! With one hand upon the gas and another tweaking her nipples, he focussed straight ahead, his eyes scanning the horizon. Occasionally, he looked at her and gave a smile.

'Do you like it up here, Elizabeth?'

She smiled. 'Very much, Mr Darcy.'

'Watch this.' Mr Darcy approached the edge of the basket, where the sandbags were attached.

'I'm going to drop one!' he announced, his lips quirked up into a wicked smile.

'Pray, do not do that!' Elizabeth shrieked.

With a flick of his hand, Mr Darcy released a sandbag. The balloon suddenly jolted higher towards the sun and Elizabeth's stomach somersaulted. She smiled up at him – he looked so young, so carefree.

'Would *you* like to be in control just this once, Elizabeth?' he asked, his grey eyes dancing with humour. 'You may steer Charlie Tango, if you like.'

Elizabeth was flummoxed. 'How … how does it work?' she asked nervously.

'Well, all hot-air balloons operate on a simple scientific principle,' explained Mr Darcy. 'Warm air rises in cooler air. Essentially, hot air is lighter than cool air, because it has less mass per unit of volume, and therefore the buoyant force acting upon the balloon keeps it afloat. Are you following me?'

Elizabeth nodded.

'You can understand the process by thinking of Archimedes' Principle: any body completely or partially submerged in a fluid is buoyed up by a force equal to the weight of the fluid displaced by the body.'

'I meant,' Elizabeth interrupted, 'is there a joystick or anything?'

'Oh. No, you just open and close this thing,' Mr Darcy said, indicating the control on the hydrogen burner. He leant down and unclasped the buckles that bound her hands.

Elizabeth grasped the control eagerly and flames shot up into the canopy overhead.

'Whoa, go easy, baby!' Mr Darcy exclaimed in a very un-nineteenth-century way. 'You only need a light touch.' Elizabeth quickly adjusted her grip. The balloon steadied and soared at her command, rising and dipping through the cool morning air.

'On, now off. On, and off,' Mr Darcy guided her as she fired up and turned off the gas. He smiled at her, his eyes bright. 'Good girl,' he said sexily. Or patronizingly, depending on your point of view.

'Do you know,' he murmured, 'what the Quarter-of-a-

Mile High Club is, Elizabeth?'

Elizabeth shook her head. 'I confess, I have no idea, Mr Darcy.'

Mr Darcy's exquisite lips quirked up. 'Members of the Quarter-of-a-Mile High Club have endeavoured to enjoy the act of love while airborne.'

Elizabeth was puzzled. 'But hot-air balloons are such a new invention,' she remarked. 'I was led to believe not many women have ever travelled in them.'

Mr Darcy looked discomfited. 'It is true that on many of the first manned flights, the balloonists took animals – principally sheep – with them, to test the effects of altitude.'

Elizabeth's eyes widened. 'So they …?'

'Who knows, Elizabeth.' Mr Darcy cut in. 'But the principle is appealing, is it not?'

His grey eyes bored into hers. Elizabeth would have squirmed under his scrutiny, but, bound as she was by so many restraints, she could barely move her limbs.

'Have you ever … ' She steeled herself to ask the question. 'Have you ever brought Lady Catherine up here?'

'No, Elizabeth,' he said in a low voice. 'This is a first for me.'

'And Lady Catherine, has she ever slept in a bedchamber with you?'

'Never. I do not think she would want me to see her without her make-up and her prosthetics.'

'Prosthetics?' Elizabeth was curious.

'Chicken fillets, Elizabeth,' Mr Darcy explained patiently. 'She uses them to enhance her bosom.'

Elizabeth would have hugged herself with joy, had Mr Darcy not just re-pinioned her arms back to her sides. So Lady Catherine's bubbies were not so magnificent after all!

'Pemberley!' Mr Darcy suddenly shouted, and pointed east. 'Look, Elizabeth, do you see?'

In the far distance, Elizabeth could just make out a grand house of pale stone, with landscaped grounds, set against a bank of purple-tinged hills.

'It is truly breathtaking!' she gasped. It was at least three times the size of Netherfield, and far exceeded that property in elegance. 'But how have we arrived here so soon? We left Hertfordshire barely an hour ago.'

'It was imperative that we made haste,' Mr Darcy replied. 'Readers are at risk of becoming restless. Now we are at Pemberley we can get on with the truly filthy bits.'

'Could you sign the visitors' book?' Mr Darcy asked Elizabeth as they entered the imposing marble-clad lobby. Elizabeth gazed around in wonder, blushing at the ceiling-high frescos of nuns beating each other with wimples. Such grandeur, and such … *individual* taste!

'Of course,' she remarked, 'I would be delighted to.'

Mr Darcy held out the book, along with a quill pen.

'Lovely setting,' she wrote hastily. 'Great weather. I am sure we'll have a super time.'

'Ha!' Mr Darcy said triumphantly, snapping the book shut. 'You have just signed my non-disclosure agreement, Miss Bennet.'

'Whatever do you mean, Mr Darcy?'

'It is a legally binding contract that forbids you from mentioning to anyone what goes on at Pemberley.'

Elizabeth swallowed nervously. Just what *did* go on at Pemberley? Despite her misgivings, she endeavoured to sound bold. 'So, you have my word that I will remain silent. Does this mean you intend to make love to me tonight, Mr Darcy?'

'Let us be clear, Miss Bennet, I do not make love,' Mr

Darcy said coolly. 'I bonk. I have it off. I get my end away. I roger. I boff.'

Elizabeth's pulse quickened. *Bonking! Jeez, that sounded so ... hot.*

'Secondly, there is much to do before we can consider your initiation. You need food, and rest. Allow me to show you to your room.'

Mr Darcy crossed the lobby and ascended the main staircase, then turned right into a corridor, with Elizabeth following behind. They passed several doors until they reached one at the end. Beyond it was a small bedchamber with an expansive bed. Everything in the room was white – the furniture, walls and bedding. It was sterile and cold but with the most glorious views of Seattle through the glass wall. Which was most puzzling, seeing as they were in Derbyshire.

'This will be your room, Miss Bennet,' Mr Darcy said with a sweep of his hand. 'You may add any furnishings that you see fit.'

'Will you ...' Elizabeth hesitated. 'Will you be sharing my bedchamber, Mr Darcy?'

'No, Elizabeth, I will not. As you know, I do not sleep with anyone – apart from my cuddly toys. Now come, you must be hungry.'

'I am fully aware that this is a dark path I'm leading you down, Elizabeth,' said Mr Darcy, leading her down a dark path through the shrubbery towards the kitchen wing. 'You must undoubtedly have some questions about the sub/dom scene.'

Elizabeth blushed. 'I confess, I have so little knowledge of the matters of which you speak, I know not what to ask.'

'Oh, Elizabeth ...' he sighed. 'You are such an innocent. A sweet, innocent flower, ready to be plucked. And I can wait no longer. I must pluck you tonight.'

Mr Darcy sexily opened the door to the main kitchen and stepped aside to let her pass through it. Inside a fair-haired woman – presumably the cook – was sweating vegetables over the stove.

'Oh, good day, Mr Darcy,' she said cheerfully, mopping some swede and broccoli from her brow.

'Good day, Mrs Jones,' Mr Darcy said warmly. 'You may attend to your other duties. I shall prepare Miss Bennet's repast myself.'

'As you wish, Sir.' Mrs Jones gave a brief curtsey and, stooping to pick up some carrots that had dripped from her underarms, hurried out of the room.

'She is a medical oddity,' Mr Darcy explained, filling a pot with water and setting it upon the stove top to boil, 'and yet a most efficient housekeeper.' Disappearing into the pantry, he emerged attractively with a packet of Tangy Cheese Doritos and a boil-in-the-bag chicken curry.

'Ha! *Not* gay!' triumphed her Inner Slapper.

'I do have one question,' Elizabeth ventured. 'How did you become this way? Was it at Beaton that your interest in pain and humiliation began?'

Mr Darcy dropped the curry into the pan of water in a really sexy way.

'Why is anyone the way they are?' he mused, shaking Doritos into a bowl and placing it in front of Elizabeth. 'Please, help yourself.'

'I seem to have lost my appetite, Mr Darcy.'

'Eat!'

Reluctantly, Elizabeth took a handful of crisps.

'Is it easy to find young ladies who wish to ... to indulge your fantasies?'

'Let me see. There was Dolly and Molly. Then Polly. Then Kitty and Mariah, Harriet, Juliana, Mary and Charlotte, then Sven – that was a bit of a departure for me – then Emma, Augusta and Amelia.'

'So many!' gasped Elizabeth.

'You have no need to be jealous, Miss Bennet,' he said ardently, gazing intently upon her features. 'There is something special about you. You have bewitched me.' His steel-grey eyes were hungry, like the wolf.

Suddenly, he slammed his fist upon the table.

'Eat up your bloody Doritos, Elizabeth!'

Elizabeth gave a start. He was so changeable!

'I have another question,' she blurted out, spraying Doritos crumbs across the flagstone floor. 'Do you intend to hurt me?'

Mr Darcy looked grave. 'I shall punish you, Elizabeth. And yes, it will hurt. But I will start gently. Tonight, I shall merely hump you – hard.'

He took a step forward and seized her in his arms. Elizabeth could feel the length of his body against hers, as he gently unpinned her hair with one hand, fixed it into a funky, low-slung ponytail and gave it a quick squirt of hairspray. *'Et voila!'* he trilled.

Wow, he was so good with hair and stuff!

He leant down and held her, forcefully, pressing his manhood against her womanhood. 'Let me roger you, Elizabeth,' he breathed. 'I want to stick it in you. I want to stick it in you and wiggle it about.'

Oh my! He spoke so eloquently, so urgently, that Elizabeth felt all resistance melting away.

'Yes! Yes! Take me now!' she said huskily.

Mr Darcy took her by the hand, and led her back through the kitchen door, through the shrubbery, in through the side door to the East Wing, up the main staircase, across the gallery to the West Wing, and down a corridor to the left. Then down another staircase, past the nursery and left again into an anteroom.

'Do you still want to do this, Elizabeth?' he asked, looking searchingly into her eyes.

'I must confess, I am going slightly off the boil,' she answered.

'Then we have no time to lose.'

Together they hurried down another corridor to the right, up a narrow staircase, and down another corridor, and finally, in through the door to his bedchamber. *Holy crap, it was vast!* The room was dominated by an enormous four-poster bed, hung with a red silk canopy. Beside it was a red leather chaise longue, a red leather pouffe and a red leather console table. On the ceiling was a painting of Poseidon the sea god, poking a naked woman with his trident.

Slowly, sexily, Mr Darcy removed his pocket watch and placed it carefully on the console table beside the bed. He shrugged off his tailcoat, folded it neatly and laid it upon the pouffe.

'I have waited so long for this moment, Miss Bennet,' he breathed. Carefully, he removed his cravat and linen shirt, ironed them, sprayed them with lavender laundry spray and added them to the pile. Next it was the turn of his breeches. *Holy flip!* Elizabeth gazed down at the floor as he removed them, and when she found the courage to look up, he was almost naked. *Oh my!* He was heart-stoppingly beautiful. Apart from one thing.

Elizabeth swallowed nervously.

'Will you not take off your stockings and garters, Mr Darcy?'

'I have chilblains, Elizabeth,' he complained, sexily. His eyes narrowed, and his Adam's apple throbbed. 'Now it is your turn,' he murmured.

Mr Darcy moved towards her with feline grace, like a jungle cat – crawling on all fours, waving his tail and making yowling noises. Arriving at her feet, he paused and gazed upwards.

'My God, I am going to give you a seeing-to, Elizabeth Bennet,' he growled. 'I shall bang you into the middle of next week.'

Elizabeth closed her eyes in longing. Her most unmentionable body parts were now throbbing in anticipation; desire filled every fibre of her being.

Grabbing at her dress, Mr Darcy slowly pulled himself up, using her body as leverage.

'Oof!' he puffed.

Now he was towering over her, his grey eyes swimming with desire.

'Turn round,' he ordered.

Elizabeth turned, and felt Mr Darcy's hands deftly undoing the buttons of her gown. Slowly, teasingly, he pulled it over her head. He shook it out, then fetched a hanger from the wardrobe and suspended the dress from it. 'Hmm, what's that?' he mused, scratching at a small stain on the hem.

'Ink, I believe.'

'You should try soaking that in milk,' he suggested. 'If that doesn't work, rub it with some lye soap.'

God, he was such a perfectionist!

He turned back to Elizabeth and gazed upon her near-naked loveliness.

'I'm going to boff you now, Miss Bennet,' he declared. 'Hard. You had better brace yourself.'

Apprehension suddenly seized her. She was unsure of what to do, how to move. Would he be disappointed? As if sensing her thoughts, Mr Darcy took control.

'Lie down on the bed, Elizabeth,' he commanded, 'and lift up your shift.'

Gingerly, she lay back upon the red embroidered quilt.

'Why, Miss Bennet, are those my longjohns?' he asked in surprise. His brow furrowed. 'We had better remove them at once. I'd been wearing them for five days straight.'

Quickly, he ripped the worsted leggings from her slender legs, and paused, drinking in her milky whiteness.

'Prepare yourself, Madam, for your first taste of nooky,' he said huskily, clambering onto the bed beside her.

Jeez, he was so beautiful! She reached out a hand to caress him.

'No touching!' Mr Darcy gasped.

Why? *Why* couldn't she touch him? He was so exquisite, it was impossible to resist. Determinedly, Elizabeth grasped his manhood with her delicate fingers. Mr Darcy flinched. Then his body quivered uncontrollably, and suddenly – *oh my!* – there was an emission that, were it to be named, would be bound to soil the pages of this book.

'Nooooooo!' groaned Mr Darcy.

'Oh!' exclaimed Elizabeth.

Mr Darcy's eyes grew dark, and his mouth set in a grim line.

'I said, "no touching", Elizabeth.'

'Forgive me!' Elizabeth was mortified. 'I did not know what might happen!'

'Dammit, Elizabeth. I am a man of uncontrollable passions!' Mr Darcy cried. 'I am constantly in a state of arousal. Especially with you. Do you remember that first evening, at Netherfield, when I refused to dance? The truth was, I was in such a sexual frenzy at seeing your fine, ripe bubbies barely constrained by that thin cotton gown you wore, that had I been forced to perform as much as a *pas de chat*, my breeches would have exploded.

'People believe I am proud, and haughty,' he continued, 'when in fact I am constantly on the verge of release. A little stiffness and formality in manner is only to be expected when one is endeavouring not to reach the point of no return in polite company.'

'Perhaps,' Elizabeth ventured, 'if you dwelt a little less on sexual congress, and diverted your attention occasionally towards less titillating pursuits ...'

He gave a harsh laugh. 'Like lacemaking, perhaps?'

'Is it such a strange idea? You may find such activities have a soothing effect upon your libido, and your ... problem ... may not trouble you so.'

Mr Darcy leant upon one elbow, and traced the contours of Elizabeth's face with his freaky fingers. 'Oh, Miss Bennet, you are so innocent,' he sighed. His expression hardened. 'I am no good for you. You should keep away from me.'

'Wait a minute, *you* invited *me* here.'

'Whatever. I am too insatiable, too kinky for you.'

'Try me.'

'You don't know what you're asking, Elizabeth,' he groaned.

'Mr Darcy ... Fitzwilliam ... I would like to know the real you. Please – let me in.'

Mr Darcy was lost in thought for a moment. Then he seemed to make a decision.

'Come, Elizabeth. I am going to show you something that will make you wish you had never come to Pemberley.'

It was with evident pride that Mr Darcy led Elizabeth about the finest rooms at Pemberley. There were stately galleries, elegant parlours and lofty bedchambers, all with magnificent views of the parkland beyond, and all lavishly decorated with sex-themed accessories. Everywhere Elizabeth looked were phallic vases, breast-shaped cushions and furry rugs that looked just like vulvas. Mr Darcy observed Elizabeth's face closely, seeming to take delight in her mortification; he was particularly pleased to see her blush scarlet at the frescos of young men in fetish gear in The Old Queen's Bedroom. And yet during the tour, Mr Darcy discussed the interior decor with such enthusiasm and knowledge – pointing out pelmets newly imported from France, and the exquisite detailing on the marquetry cabinets – that once again Elizabeth wondered whether he might be homosexual. *Holy crap, he was so complicated!*

At last, exiting the ballroom – which was gaudily decorated with gilded testicles – Elizabeth allowed herself to be guided by Mr Darcy through a side door and into a narrow wood-panelled corridor. Unlike the handsomely proportioned room they had just left, it was dark and almost menacing, with no window of any kind to let in light and no portraits or other decoration enlivening the bare walls. In the dim light, Elizabeth could just discern a door at the end of the corridor, painted black or darkest blue, and adorned with a single ornate brass handle.

'It is a magnificent knob, is it not?' Mr Darcy remarked, raising one eyebrow. 'I find when it comes to opening things up, a larger knob is far superior to a small one. And it is so much more satisfying to grasp.'

Elizabeth sighed. If Mr Darcy's 'problem' was ever to be overcome, then she would have to discourage this manner of conversation. She had had to throw a glass of water over him earlier in the scullery, when he had become overexcited pointing out a pair of particularly fine enormous jugs.

'Mr Darcy, I have no particular wish to discourse about

doorknobs, whatever their size,' she exclaimed, her cheeks aglow. 'I implore you to return to the subject at hand. You promised to show me your favourite room.'

With a sudden whirling movement, Mr Darcy turned and gripped her arms fiercely. His eyes smouldered like hot coals in the darkness.

'Yes, Elizabeth, you have seen all the rooms at Pemberley. All – except one,' he said huskily. In such close proximity, Elizabeth could feel Mr Darcy's hot breath on her skin, and smell his distinctive scent of animal musk and cheap supermarket body wash. She felt her knees giving way beneath her.

Just as suddenly, Mr Darcy released her. A wicked grin lit up his chiselled face. Stretching out one of his extraordinarily long index fingers five or six feet to the end of the corridor, he caressed the paintwork of the door lovingly.

'Yes, there is another room,' Mr Darcy murmured, 'the one closest to my heart – if indeed I possess such a thing. I show it only to those who intrigue me. Only those who I believe capable of' – his eyes were truly blazing now, blowing out little puffs of smoke as they locked on to Elizabeth's – '*pleasing* me.'

Elizabeth wilted under his gaze, like a six-day-old lettuce. 'Pleasing you?'

'Oh, Elizabeth …' His index finger brushed her top lip. *Crap, if only she'd shaved this morning!* 'Little, innocent Lizzy. What you saw in the Purple Pantry of Pleasure was nothing. My Lilac Library of Licentiousness is intended to but whet the appetite. This is where my true desires lie.'

With that, Mr Darcy grasped the knob in his manly hands and thrust open the door. He smiled, and his grey eyes shot flames of desire towards hers, singeing her fringe and eyebrows.

'Welcome,' he announced, 'to my Blue Broom Cupboard of Seriously Kinky Shit!'

At first, Elizabeth could discern little of the contents therein; in the dim light, she was aware only of dark shapes – some long and narrow, others broader and more robust – outlined against the back wall of the cupboard. But as her eyes became accustomed to the darkness, details began to leap out at her: the spikes of a scrubbing brush, the curves of a tennis racket.

She gave a little gasp.

'You like what you see, Miss Bennet?'

Mr Darcy was immediately behind her now, his warm breath caressing her bare neck.

Elizabeth's own breathing was ragged. Every one of her senses was heightened; she felt giddy, as if she were on the edge of a cliff, looking down. Attached to gilded hooks set into the cupboard walls were instruments of every kind of punishment. Wooden spoons in various sizes. Fearsome-looking hairbrushes. Ping-pong bats, curtain tie-backs; she could even make out a monstrously large carpet beater. Their appearance was at once menacing and yet, in some strange way, thrilling.

Her eyes fell upon one particularly terrifying-looking instrument: a long red stick, at the top of which were affixed scores of grey, rope-like tendrils. Elizabeth blanched.

'What, pray, is that?' she asked in a whisper.

Mr Darcy shrugged. 'Oh, that's just a mop. I think one of the servants must have left it here.'

He leant past her and from one of the hooks, took down a slim, bristled brush.

'We shall start gently, Elizabeth,' he said huskily, caressing the bristles of the brush between his long index fingers. 'You deserve to be punished for your repeated impertinence and wilfulness, but I shall deliver no more pain than you can withstand. You are, after all, an innocent.'

Elizabeth's legs trembled. *Holy flip, what was he planning?*

'Kneel, Elizabeth,' Mr Darcy commanded. His whole body seemed to throb with desire, and Elizabeth, as if in a trance, did as she was bid. She knew not why, but she felt powerless to resist.

'Now, bend over, on all fours.'

Shakily, Elizabeth complied.

At once, Mr Darcy's strong hands were upon her, seizing her gown and petticoat at the hem and tugging them up, hard – oh, the disgrace! – to expose her stocking tops and bare derriere. Elizabeth flushed scarlet, and her breath came in little gasps.

She felt Mr Darcy's palm caress the curve of her behind.

'Oh, Elizabeth,' he murmured. 'You are truly callipygous.'

'Calli-what?' she breathed.

'It's Greek, Elizabeth. It means you have a fantastic arse.' *Wow, he knew so much about stuff!*

Suddenly, Mr Darcy ceased his ministrations. 'Enough!' he barked. His tone had changed, and Elizabeth guessed that fondling was no longer his intention.

'I am going to beat you with this toothbrush, Miss Bennet,' Mr Darcy said huskily. 'It will hurt, but you must show forbearance.'

Elizabeth girded her loins, awaiting the blow.

There was a tantalizing pause, and then – *pfft!* – Mr Darcy brought the toothbrush down on Elizabeth's quivering flesh.

'Again!' Mr Darcy cried, and twice more the toothbrush grazed Elizabeth's behind.

'Is that good, Elizabeth?' Mr Darcy asked, panting now.

'Um …' Elizabeth was uncertain how to respond without causing Mr Darcy distress. 'I can't really feel anything much.'

'What, nothing?'

'It kind of tickles, I suppose.'

'Oh!' Mr Darcy sounded deflated. He squeezed past her and rummaged in the broom cupboard for a minute or so, emerging with a devilish grin, brandishing a folded-up copy of the *London Gazette*.

'I see we are going to have to be strict with you, Miss Bennet,' he said lasciviously. 'You evidently have a stronger constitution than I credited. Prepare yourself!'

Pat! The newspaper flopped against her derriere.

'Maybe if you rolled it up?' suggested Elizabeth.

'A wicked notion, Miss Bennet!' Mr Darcy murmured. 'I heartily approve.'

There was a pause while Mr Darcy unfolded the newspaper, then rolled it into a thick stubby wand. Then unfolded it again and rolled it, more carefully this time, into a long, thin wand.

Phtatt! Mr Darcy swung the newspaper against Elizabeth's flesh.

'My God, Elizabeth!' he moaned, breathing heavily.

Phtatt! Phtatt! Phtatt! Mr Darcy's breathing was ragged now. 'Feel it, Elizabeth!' he groaned. 'Give it to me!'

Give what *to him?* Elizabeth wondered, feeling both mystified and slightly embarrassed. To be honest, this wasn't really doing anything for her at all.

'Come for me, baby!' Mr Darcy said in a strangled whisper.

Unsure of the ways of the flesh, Elizabeth plundered her memory for the only act of love she had ever witnessed: a bull tupping a cow on a neighbour's farm. Tentatively, she let out a long, low 'Mooooooo!'

'Yes!!! My God, Lizzy!' Mr Darcy cried in ecstasy, dropping to his knees. The newspaper wand fell limply from his grasp.

When Elizabeth awoke the next morning in unfamiliar surroundings, for a moment she could not recollect where she was. Then fleeting remembrances of the evening before leapt, unbidden, into her mind.

She was at Pemberley, in her new bedchamber. And – *oh my!* – Fitzwilliam Darcy had flogged her with a toothbrush, and a newspaper!

Elizabeth turned over in bed, burying her face in the pillow. Perhaps if she fell asleep again, she would awaken at Longbourn, and the events of the previous evening would all prove to be nothing but a dream. While she lay dozing, she felt, rather than heard, the door open, and realized at once that there was someone else in the room.

'I have taken the liberty of bringing you some breakfast.'

Fitzwilliam Darcy, his lithe, muscly form clad in white pantaloons and a close-fitting vest, stood beside her bed with a tray laden with buttered buns, eggs, muffins, two blancmanges, a plum pudding, a flagon of ale and a roast rib of beef.

'How are you feeling this morning?'

'Quite well, thank you, Sir.' Elizabeth's gaze met his, but as ever, she was unable to divine what he was thinking. Those steel-grey eyes of his were impenetrable.

Mr Darcy set down the tray on the edge of the bed.

'It is nine o'clock, Miss Bennet,' he said sternly.

'Have you been up long, Mr Darcy?'

'Indeed I have. I rose early this morning, in order to perform physical jerks with Taylor.'

Elizabeth merely nodded.

'I am, in fact, about to do my ablutions. You may, should you desire, give yourself a good scrub down with a flannel.' He indicated a pitcher of water set upon the dresser. 'You are a *very dirty girl.*

Evidently, there was to be no abatement in Mr Darcy's ardour. Yesterday's activities had but whetted his appetite for more.

Mr Darcy perched upon the bedclothes and unfurled one of his long index fingers. Gently, he stroked Elizabeth's hand.

'I'd like to bite those nails,' he murmured darkly.

Oh my! Beneath the heavy bedclothes, Elizabeth squirmed in a most unladylike fashion.

Suddenly, Mr Darcy appeared distracted, and he stood and walked briskly towards the door.

'You will find some new clothes at the end of the bed,' he said, turning in the doorway. 'I would advise you to put them all on. It will be cold where we are going.'

'And where, pray, might that be?' Elizabeth asked apprehensively.

Mr Darcy's face was, once again, impassive. 'Today, Miss Bennet, I am going to take you up the Peakshole.'

At length, Elizabeth dressed and curled her hair under a beribboned blue bonnet that someone – presumably Mrs Jones or one of the maidservants – had provided. Mr Darcy himself was waiting for her at the bottom of the staircase, dressed in a billowing white shirt and tight breeches.

'Good morning, Miss Bennet,' he said gravely. 'You look most becoming.'

Proffering his arm, he led her out onto the terrace in front of the house, from where she could see the Derbyshire Peaks laid out before her. She and Mr Darcy circled round to the left and passed through a gate in a low wall to the kitchen garden, and from there proceeded to the rose arbour and the topiary garden, on to the tea rooms and back round through the gift shop – *holy heck, the grounds were vast!* – finally emerging onto a lawn which led down to a wide, fast-flowing stream. A black-painted barge was moored there, secured to a tree stump, and within it, at the back, were seated three men of middling age carrying fiddles and a drum. Painted on the side of the barge, in gold lettering, was what Elizabeth presumed must be the barge's name: SUV.

'Step aboard, Miss Bennet,' said Mr Darcy, bowing ceremoniously and holding out his hand. Elizabeth took it and, as she did so, a jolt of electricity shot through her body. Damn her plastic flip-flops!

'Sit!' Mr Darcy directed her to a chair, set facing the stern. There were buckles and ropes of every length dangling from its sides. Mr Darcy knelt before her, and carefully wrapped one of the ropes about her waist, tying it at the back of the chair. He looked up and smiled. Another strap he buckled about her arms, pinioning her to the chair back, while two more ropes bound her hands behind her back. Darcy fastened her ankles to the chair legs with a thick cord, and finally, inserted a ball gag into her mouth.

'All safely strapped in, Miss Bennet? Then we are ready to sail.'

Elizabeth watched in wonder as Mr Darcy deftly handled the rudder, guiding the barge out into midstream. It was thrilling! Her heart raced in her chest as the trees and riverbanks flew by at 0.003 miles per hour. Mr Darcy's face was a mask of concentration. Just one wrong turn of the rudder and they might veer slightly to the left or to the right, or even bump into a floating log. *Oh my!* Her fate lay in Mr Darcy's hands!

'Mmmmf mf mmmmfff ummf fuf?' she enquired.

'Sorry?'

'Mmmmfff...'

'Just a sec.' Mr Darcy leant over and removed the ball gag from Elizabeth's mouth.

'I beg your pardon, Miss Bennet?'

'Where did you learn to sail, Mr Darcy?'

'Oh, I've been coming up the Peakshole since I was a boy, Miss Bennet,' he replied gaily. 'The river runs through the Pemberley estate, and on through the village of Bumswell.'

'And those gentlemen at the back? Are they villagers returning thither?'

Mr Darcy looked amused. 'No, Miss Bennet. They are my in-boat music system.' He turned his smoky-grey eyes upon the musicians and barked, 'Play!'

Hastily they picked up their instruments, and began at once the first notes of a jaunty air.

Elizabeth looked puzzled. 'I am not familiar with this tune. Pray, what is it?'

'It is by Mozart, part of his Horn Concerto.'

Elizabeth listened to the music in silence for some time, staring out over the sun-dappled water.

'I must ask, also, Mr Darcy,' she said eventually, 'is this scene in Miss Austen's book?'

'No, it's in the other one,' said Mr Darcy with a wry smile. 'Its purpose, I believe, is to further reveal what a capable, suave, all-knowing alpha male I am, and cast light upon your own helplessness and general ignorance about everything from sex to classical music.'

'I see,' replied Elizabeth gravely. 'But what of my general clumsiness? It has not been illustrated for some chapters now. One might say it has become almost an afterthought.'

They both pondered in silence for several moments. 'Do you think I should fall in?' asked Elizabeth.

Mr Darcy frowned. 'I do not favour the idea, Elizabeth.

It is very dangerous. You may get injured.'

'I would get very, very wet,' said Elizabeth teasingly.

'You would.'

'And my gown would become completely see-through.'

Mr Darcy's eyes glistened with lust. 'Undoubtedly.'

He reached over and began untying her restraints. 'Whatever am I going to do with you, Miss Bennet?' he murmured. 'Sweet, accident-prone Lizzy.' And picking her up in his sexy arms, he heaved her over the side.

'My God! Elizabeth!' he cried in anguish, as the water closed over her head. Before she knew what was happening, his strong arms had grasped her about the waist. He had dived in after her! She felt a tug as he dragged her upwards, and they both surfaced, she spluttering, he grim-faced and angry.

'What in damnation do you think you're playing at?' he cried, water dripping sexily off his copper curls. 'These waters are dangerous, Lizzy!'

With an almighty shove, he pushed her back into the safety of the barge, and effortlessly pulled himself up after her. His face was furious, his eyes radiating pain and concern.

'I thought I'd lost you!' he growled. 'You must promise me, you must never, *never* go near water again.'

Elizabeth squeezed water from her sodden gown. 'What if I need a bath?' she asked meekly.

'Two inches of water only!' Mr Darcy snapped. *Oh boy, he was really riled now!*

They sat in silence for the return journey, and Mr Darcy glowered sexily all the way. The water had, as planned, caused Elizabeth's gown to lose its opacity, and Mr Darcy's eyes never left her figure. As soon as they set foot upon the bank, Mr Darcy began to drag her up the lawn towards the house.

'It's time, Elizabeth,' he said firmly.

'Time for what, Mr Darcy?'

'Your seeing-to. Come ...'

Elizabeth hesitated just a little too long. Mr Darcy's grey eyes grew steely and dark.

'Are you being wilful? You are not intending to disobey me again, are you, Elizabeth?'

Jeez, he was intense. 'No,' Elizabeth replied in a small voice.

'No, what?'

'What?'

'No, *what*?'

'What?! What don't I know?'

'No, I mean, you're supposed to say, "Sir".'

'Oh, sorry,' Elizabeth replied, flustered. 'Um, no, *Sir.*'

Mr Darcy appeared relieved. 'That's better. Now, follow me. It's nookie time.'

Elizabeth lay on Mr Darcy's bed, staring up at the kinky painting that adorned the ceiling. Her wrists were secured to the bedposts with lengths of satin ribbon, her ankles tied in the same way. Naked, helpless, she was Mr Darcy's plaything, ready for him to toy with. *Jeez, this was hot!*

Mr Darcy appeared at the foot of the bed. His chest was naked, his muscles rippling in the candlelight. On his lower body he wore a pair of ripped riding breeches, and in his hands he brandished a basket of foodstuffs he'd gathered from the kitchen.

His expression was carnal, his eyes hooded and full of longing. Slowly, mesmerizingly slowly, he walked round the side of the bed, drinking in the sight of Elizabeth's naked loveliness. Suddenly, his hand swung out and –

splat! – he flung an overripe tomato at her breast. Elizabeth gave a little cry of surprise. The tomato juice dripped down over her nipple and onto the bedclothes, and at once she was lost, lost in a sea of sensation.

Which of his comestibles would come next? Her nerve endings tingled in expectation, and she let out a low moan.

'Silence!' Mr Darcy commanded. *Flump! Flump!* Two handfuls of jam sponge landed on her other breast. *Whump!* She jolted as a cabbage bounced off her pubic hair.

'You are mine, Lizzy,' Mr Darcy said in an expressionless voice. 'Mine, to punish and humiliate.' *Splot!* An egg exploded just below her navel.

Mr Darcy moved over to the dresser and picked up a pitcher of water. Edging back towards the bed, he hurled its contents into Elizabeth's face. The shock of the water made her gasp. *Holy twat, it was cold!* Rivulets of water coursed through her hair and dripped onto the pillow beneath.

'Oh baby, let me feel how wet you are!' Mr Darcy murmured, running his hand through Elizabeth's soaking mane. 'Mmm, so wet, just for me …'

Elizabeth gave another moan. There was water up her nose and in her ears, but all she could feel was Mr Darcy's probing fingers and the heat of those passionate eyes.

Mr Darcy's hands strayed further down, down to Elizabeth's aching breasts. Gently, sensuously, he rubbed jam and cake crumbs all over her skin.

'Taste!' he ordered, holding one of his long index fingers in front of her lips. Duly, she opened her mouth and sucked.

'Is that good, Elizabeth?'

'Mmmm …' she murmured appreciatively. She loved sponge fingers.

Abruptly, Mr Darcy rose and stepped back. She could hear his breathing becoming more ragged as he reached down into his basket and pulled out an enormous, gnarled parsnip.

'This is what naughty girls get,' he rasped, holding the parsnip reverently in both hands.

With one swift movement, he tore the ribbons binding Elizabeth's feet. Instinctively, she raised her legs up, out of harm's way.

'A nice try, Miss Bennet,' Mr Darcy murmured. 'But there is to be no escaping your punishment.'

His mouth set into a hard line, and his eyes darkened. Raising his arm, he brought the vegetable down firmly, painfully, on Elizabeth's exposed behind.

'Oww!' she gasped. She had never been beaten with a vegetable before, and it was surprisingly painful.

Again and again, Mr Darcy thwacked his parsnip against Elizabeth's behind, again and again, up and down. It seemed he would never stop. Faster and faster it rose and fell; Elizabeth's flesh felt hot and raw.

'Come on, Elizabeth, let go!' Mr Darcy groaned, his parsnip vibrating with each urgent stroke, his eyes closed in ecstasy. With every effort of strength, Elizabeth wriggled free from the ribbons that bound her hands. This time, she *would* touch him, she determined. She would show him exactly what a loving embrace felt like. Her hands travelled down, further down, until they reached Mr Darcy's breeches. Closing about his taut buttocks, she pulled his body firmly towards hers.

'Oh, Elizabeth … Mind my plums!' Mr Darcy cried out. There was a horrible squelching noise, and Elizabeth felt juice trickling between her fingers.

'You've squashed my plums!' Mr Darcy cried, disbelief etched upon his handsome features. 'My special kinky-sex breeches are totally ruined now!'

Mortified, Elizabeth saw that two overripe plums, which Mr Darcy had been keeping in reserve in his back pockets, had been quite flattened by her eager hands.

Mr Darcy was angry now, truly angry. 'I told you, Elizabeth, never to touch me! Can you not follow that one simple rule?'

'I am so sorry,' she said meekly. 'I am sure I can get the stains out of your breeches if you just allow me to try.'

Mr Darcy scowled. 'Never mind my damn breeches. Jones will take care of them. The point is, why are you so wilful? Why can you not simply obey me, like a true submissive would?'

Elizabeth looked down. 'I … I am beginning to doubt that I have what it takes to be a submissive,' she said, not daring to look up into his blazing grey eyes. 'I am not sure I enjoy being pelted with vegetables, or tied up, or whacked with newspapers. I want other things.'

'Other things?' Mr Darcy's eyes widened in horror and alarm. 'Do you mean icky, yucky stuff, like holding hands?'

'And maybe kissing sometimes. And just hugging, without you attempting to feel me up at the same time.'

'But this is the way I am, Elizabeth. I am not sure I can do those things. My time at Beaton …' His voice trailed off, and he looked so young, so damaged, that Elizabeth felt her heart flood with tenderness. 'I was never kissed, never hugged. I was flogged daily, and learnt to love it, as I'm sure you will too if you give it a chance.'

Elizabeth shook her head. She was unsure what to think. Was she capable of saving this sexy aristo with the smouldering grey eyes and fucked-up personality? Or was he just an irredeemable perv, beyond anyone's reach?

'Please just tell me one thing,' she said, wiping tomato juice off her breasts. 'What is it with you and food?'

Mr Darcy sat on the edge of the bed, seemingly oblivious now to the plum juice that dripped from his breeches. 'You've probably wondered why there are no portraits of me as a youth at Pemberley,' he said quietly. 'That's because, when I was a child, I was a great big fatso.'

Elizabeth was shocked. Mr Darcy – obese? But he was *so freakin' hot!* How was it possible?

'Quite simply, I was greedy, Elizabeth. Just as now I am greedy for female flesh, during my schooldays I was greedy for cream cakes and steamed puddings. I wobbled when I walked. The other boys at Beaton called me "Fatzwilliam".'

'Then how …?' Elizabeth was thinking about Mr Darcy's washboard abs and taut buttocks.

'Lady Catherine took me in hand. She made the school put me on a strict diet, and I worked out,' he explained. 'So now, I enjoy my food vicariously. Do you understand?'

'I think so.'

'When I see you with a bacon sandwich or a hotdog, it brings me pleasure. Seeing you eat is almost as good as eating myself.'

Elizabeth could have wept. Poor Mr Darcy. Lost, fat little boy, forced to look on in the dinner hall as the other boys tucked into capons and roast mutton and rice pudding, while he partook of thin gruel. And going to bed hungry, always hungry …

'When did you last see your doctor, Elizabeth?' Mr Darcy enquired later that morning, when Elizabeth had cleaned herself up. It had taken a good while as Mr Darcy had given strict new instructions that she was to be issued with only two tablespoons of washing water per day.

'Oh, many months ago,' she replied. 'I am blessed with

robust good health.'

'Then I insist upon you seeing my physician, Dr Knowe.'

'How so? I am not feeling at all unwell. Quite the opposite, in fact.' Elizabeth's lips quirked up into a smile. *Holy hell, now she was doing it too!*

Mr Darcy's lips quirked up right back at her in amusement. 'Oh, Lizzy – my beautiful, sweet girl – how is it that you know so little of your own body? Dr Knowe is a specialist in the inner workings of women. We must take the necessary precautions to ensure that our unions do not have any unwanted results.'

'You are talking of ... a child?' Elizabeth was deeply shocked. Carried away by Mr Darcy's lusts and her own desires, she had not stopped to think of such a terrible consequence.

'Granted, it's unlikely,' her Gaydar cut in. 'He hasn't even penetrated you yet.'

'Well, yes, pregnancy is one consideration,' Mr Darcy replied, 'but mostly I want to make sure I don't give you the clap. As you know, I have frequented many bawdy houses in my time, and on one occasion, after a visit to Dirty Delilah, I did have this nasty-looking rash ...'

'Pray, do not speak of it,' said Elizabeth curtly. She could not bear to think of Mr Darcy in the arms of any woman other than herself, let alone a fifty-year-old lady of the night with a clichéd name and poor personal hygiene.

'It is a matter that we must address,' Mr Darcy said gently, taking her hand in his and looking deep into her eyes – searching, probing, like a speculum opening up a pathway to her soul. 'Dr Knowe will be here at noon. Please be ready for him.'

Elizabeth dropped her eyes. *Damn, she was even more clumsy than usual when she was flustered.* She hastily picked them up.

'I will do it for you, Fitzwilliam,' she said quietly, 'although I do not wish my most intimate parts to be seen by any man other than yourself.'

'Do not worry, Dr Knowe is an elderly man, and his sight is not what it was,' Mr Darcy explained. 'You will find him to be most tactful and discreet.'

Noon arrived, and Dr Knowe was duly greeted by Mr Darcy. He was indeed a man in the latter stages of life – about three score years and ten, Elizabeth guessed – and walked with a stoop. His manner was sprightly, however, and his wit lively, and he and Mr Darcy exchanged many pleasantries while Elizabeth waited patiently to be introduced.

'How's the old John Thomas?' asked Dr Knowe, swinging his medical bag in the direction of Mr Darcy's breeches and accidentally whacking him in the goolies. Mr Darcy doubled up and gasped for breath.

'Speak up, Darcy,' Dr Knowe entreated. 'I am old, as you well know, and my hearing is not as acute as it was in my youth.'

'It is in fine form, Doctor,' Mr Darcy panted, 'but it is to this young lady, Miss Bennet, that I wish you to minister on this occasion, not myself.'

Dr Knowe whirled about hither and thither and finally caught sight of Elizabeth.

'Good heavens, Madam, I thought you were the grandfather clock!' he exclaimed. 'A young lady, eh?' he continued. 'Then in that case, we must find somewhere more private for our little examination.' He opened the door of a nearby cabinet. 'If you will just step this way, Miss Bennet.'

'Hmmm, I'm getting a bad feeling about this,' Elizabeth's Subconscious interjected.

'Forgive me, Doctor, but that is an armoire,' Mr Darcy

pointed out.

'Good heavens, Darcy, you are right!'

'Perhaps,' Mr Darcy suggested, 'I might show you to Elizabeth's bedchamber? No one will disturb you there. Apart from Taylor, who is stationed in Miss Bennet's laundry basket.'

Elizabeth gasped. 'Taylor has been *spying* on me? Why, pray, have you asked him to do such a thing?'

Mr Darcy took Elizabeth's face in his hands, tenderly. 'To keep you safe,' he murmured. 'You might trip over a discarded ribbon. Or be knocked over by a pillow feather. I couldn't bear that to happen to you, Lizzy. You. Are. So. Precious. To. Me.'

'Are. We. Ready. To. Proceed?' asked Dr Knowe, who clearly had little time for such displays of affection.

Mr Darcy released Elizabeth and stepped back. 'Please, take good care of her, Doctor,' he entreated. His eyes were smouldering like barbecue coals. 'She belongs to me.'

'You can be assured that I will do my utmost in that regard. By the way, Darcy, when I've finished, do you want me to give you a little something for that eye infection?'

'No, thank you, Doctor. I like my eyes to smoulder. It makes me look sexy.'

The Elizabeth who emerged after an hour's probing, prodding and poking looked even more pale and wide-eyed than usual. While Doctor Knowe was packing away his instruments and conversing with Mr Darcy, she lay on a chaise longue in the parlour and tried to recover her previous good spirits. Entering into a kinky-sex pact seemingly entailed a wide and constantly changing range of humiliations and discomforts, chief among them the good Doctor 'endeavouring to locate her womb' in *completely* the wrong alleyway. She winced at the memory.

Suddenly, she found herself longing to be back at Longbourn. She wondered what Jane was doing at that very moment – picking rosemary in the garden, perhaps? Or darning her best gown? Kitty would be daydreaming, Mary would be at her pianoforte, and Lydia and Mama, no doubt, would be comparing tongue piercings. At the thought of home, Elizabeth's eyes filled with hot tears. What was she doing here, as Fitzwilliam Darcy's sex slave? Discontentedly, she turned over onto her stomach and buried her head in a plump, pale pink cushion.

'Why, Miss Bennet, that is quite an arresting sight!' Mr Darcy's voice came as if out of nowhere, his husky tones heavy with desire and anticipation.

Elizabeth lifted her head. Mr Darcy was standing over her, his grey eyes dancing with amusement. She frowned. 'What, pray, is an arresting sight?'

Mr Darcy merely smirked. Elizabeth followed his gaze down to the cushion beneath her head and realized, with a frisson of embarrassment, that it was shaped exactly like a giant pair of buttocks.

Hastily, she sat up. Why must everything at Pemberley be lewd, and wanton? Why could Mr Darcy not simply have cushion-shaped cushions, like every other gentleman?

'Oh, Elizabeth,' Mr Darcy murmured. 'Whatever are we to do? You have inflamed my desires all over again.' He reached down and caressed her cheek. 'You make me want to put on a CD of Gregorian chants and run a furry glove all over you.'

'Please, Mr Darcy,' Elizabeth entreated. 'May we not do something else this afternoon? I am greatly in need of rest.' A furry glove was the last thing she needed; she was still reeling from the parsnip-whacking.

Mr Darcy's eyes flashed in anger. His hands balled into fists at his sides. Then, just as suddenly, he seemed to relax again. *Holy psychopath, he was so changeable!*

'Very well,' he declared in a cool voice. 'We shall save the furry glove for another day. Now, come ...' He held out his hand.

'We are going somewhere?'

'If it pleases you, I should like you to meet my sister, Georgiana.'

'I should be delighted to!' Elizabeth replied. 'Are we to travel to meet her at finishing school?'

'Why, she is not at finishing school, she is here, at Pemberley,' Mr Darcy declared.

'She has just returned?'

'No, Elizabeth,' Mr Darcy smiled. 'She resides here.'

'Oh!' Elizabeth was taken by surprise. She had seen no evidence of the presence of any other persons at Pemberley, excepting the servants.

'I keep her locked in a closet for most of the time,' Mr Darcy explained. 'Oh God, no, not like *that* ...' he hastily added, seeing the look of horror upon Elizabeth's face. 'No, Georgiana is a delicate little thing, too delicate for society. She is a true innocent, sweet-tempered and gentle. I lock her up to keep her safe. She is so precious to me, and I could not bear anything to happen to her.'

Elizabeth smiled. 'I confess, I can hardly wait to meet her.'

'Then wait for me in the drawing room,' Mr Darcy replied. 'I shall go and fetch her at once.'

Elizabeth did not have to linger long. She heard footsteps thudding down the hall and a shriek of excitement, then Georgiana bowled into the room, her long dark hair flying behind her and her striking face lit up with a dazzling smile.

'Lizzy!' she exclaimed, running over to Elizabeth most indecorously and grasping her in her surprisingly strong arms. 'Fitzwilliam has told me so much about you!'

She was a tall, handsome creature, with dark eyes and strong features very much like her brother's.

'Lor, I'm desperate for a cigarette,' Georgiana cried, flinging herself down onto the chaise longue beside Elizabeth. 'I don't suppose you have one?'

Elizabeth was on the point of demurring, when Mr Darcy strode into the room.

'Now, Georgiana, do not overexcite yourself!' he cautioned. 'You do not want to have one of your turns. She is a shy little thing,' he explained to Elizabeth. 'I call her my Little Mouse.' He smiled indulgently at Georgiana.

'Jesus Christ,' Georgiana mumbled under her breath.

She turned to Elizabeth and surveyed her features. 'She is quite lovely, brother,' she exclaimed. 'Fitzwilliam has never brought a young lady here before,' she whispered into Elizabeth's ear. 'We were all convinced he was gay.'

'Tell me about it,' muttered Elizabeth's Gaydar.

'I don't suppose you and Jane have a brother, Elizabeth?' Georgiana asked, her dark eyes dancing, with tarty stilettos on. 'Some tasty sibling that I could hook up with, so that our two families and Bingley's will be involved in some sort of incestuous love triangle, or rather, love hexagon?'

'No, sadly, it never works out in real life like that,' sighed Elizabeth. 'Only in bad novels.'

'Oh well, worth a try,' said Georgiana, tossing back her black locks. She eyed Mr Darcy, who had walked to the window to survey the gardens in order to give the ladies time to exchange intimacies. Seeing that he was out of earshot, she leant closer to Elizabeth.

'Fitzwilliam tells me you know Mr Whackem,' she whispered.

Elizabeth nodded.

'Is he quite well?'

'Indeed,' replied Elizabeth. 'He is very well. He has joined the Meryton militia.'

'How I miss Jack Whackem.' Georgiana leant back against the couch with a smile. 'He is the most *fascinating* man.'

Elizabeth glanced over at Mr Darcy, who was now toying with the curtain tie-back, thwacking it against his palm. 'Your brother does not appear to share your affection.'

'Oh, that's on my account,' Georgiana said carelessly. 'Mr Whackem, you see, offered me a job at his publishing company, and Fitzwilliam could not bear the thought that I might want a life outside that bloody closet he keeps me in.'

So, Elizabeth was not the first young lady that Mr Whackem had approached regarding job opportunities? Despite herself, she could not help feeling affronted.

'What manner of employment was he offering?'

'Editorial assistant,' Georgiana replied. 'A bit of this and that. I would have started off making the tea, of course. But eventually, I would have learnt proofreading, and apparently there was a good chance of promotion after a year or so. I might have made editor.'

Elizabeth was deeply shocked. 'You speak of work so casually! You must remember that it is not a suitable pastime for a young lady of your social standing.'

'Oh, screw that!' Georgina's dark eyes flashed. She leant even further in towards Elizabeth. 'Don't you ever think that there might be more to life than playing the sodding piano and the occasional game of quoits?'

Elizabeth had to confess, she had oftimes thought the same. But no! It was a disgrace to even countenance it. A young lady's place was in the parlour or the bedchamber. Whackem had clearly put wicked ideas into Georgiana's head. No wonder Mr Darcy held him in such contempt.

'What happened in the end?' Elizabeth enquired in a low voice. 'Did you accept the job?'

'I made the mistake of leaving the contract on my bureau. Fitzwilliam found it and was furious. He forbade me to see Mr Whackem again, and bid me put all thoughts of going to New York one day and working on the Features desk at *Marie Claire* out of my head.' She sighed, and her lovely mouth quirked downwards. How like Mr Darcy she looked!

'It was for the best,' Elizabeth counselled. 'Your brother saved you from certain disgrace. To become a working girl ...' She gave an involuntary shudder. Georgiana still looked downcast, and Elizabeth took her hand.

'What will you do now?' she asked. 'Will Fitzwilliam arrange a suitable match for you?'

Georgiana rolled her eyes. 'Carrotslime Bingley wishes me to marry her brother,' she declared. Elizabeth's eyes widened. 'But he's a bit dim, don't you think? He *was* going to marry some other girl – some lower-class type, according to Carrotslime – so I thought I was safe. But Fitzwilliam told him to forget all about her and go travelling instead.'

'Your *brother* encouraged Mr Bingley to leave Netherfield?'

'Yes, he was not in favour of the match.'

Oh, poor Jane! This was too much to bear! Mr Darcy had been the means of ruining, perhaps for ever, the happiness of a most beloved sister! What a *bastard*!

Just then, Mr Darcy happened to look away from the window, and turned his gaze in Elizabeth's direction. He was looking at her with longing, his grey eyes like wire cutters, snipping away her layers of resistance. How *could* he do this?

'Maybe what he said is true,' her Subconscious cut in. 'Maybe he has no real feelings.' *God, she could be a bitch sometimes.*

There was no denying that whenever they had had occasion to speak of Jane, nothing in Mr Darcy's demeanour or manner betrayed any feelings of remorse. Elizabeth struggled to keep her composure. She did not want Georgiana to sense anything amiss. With her brother, though, she knew it would be harder to dissemble.

'Fifty shades?' her Subconscious piped up. 'Forty-nine of them seem to be "w**ker".'

In retrospect, Elizabeth knew not how she was able to sit through a morning of conversation, and a tour of Georgiana's closet, while her spirits were so dejected. She passed judgement on Georgiana's latest gowns from London when requested to do so, marvelled at the sliding mechanism of the closet door, commented politely on the decorating potential of the six foot by four foot space. Yet, all the while, her thoughts were fixated upon Jane, and how Mr Darcy had so cruelly dashed her sister's hopes. No motive could excuse his unjust and ungenerous actions. To divide a loving couple in such a manner was a torment for Mr Bingley, too; having seen him with Jane, and knowing his tender regard for her, Elizabeth could only guess at the extent of his misery and despair.

She could barely eat luncheon – despite Mr Darcy's efforts to tempt her with a Pot Noodle – and shortly afterwards excused herself and returned to her room, claiming that the excitement of meeting Georgiana had caused her to develop a headache. After barely a few minutes, Mr Darcy knocked upon the door with his sexy hands.

'Elizabeth, are you ill?' he asked, concern evident in his voice.

'Pray, leave me alone,' she exclaimed. 'I do not wish to speak to you.'

'Open this door, Elizabeth,' Mr Darcy said huskily. His ire was now raised, and Elizabeth could picture his glowering countenance.

'I shall not!' *Holy heck, she was defying Mr Darcy!* He would no doubt want to put her over his knee for this.

'Taylor?' Mr Darcy called.

Taylor climbed out of Elizabeth's laundry basket and, with an embarrassed glance in Elizabeth's direction, made his way across to the door, unlocking it from the inside. 'Just doing my job, Miss,' he said apologetically.

Mr Darcy stood in the doorway, his arms braced against the doorjamb as if he had been ready to kick his way in. His face was a mask of passion. Despite herself, Elizabeth felt a familiar pull way down in her deepest, most secret parts.

In one stride – it was a small room – Mr Darcy was at her bedside, and had seized her prone form in his hunky arms. 'If I wish to speak to you, you will speak, Miss Bennet,' he breathed. 'I am your Master, and you are my slave.' His chiselled lips were quivering with emotion and desire. Waves of cheap body wash washed over Elizabeth, making her feel heady and slightly queasy.

'I am not your slave. If you recall, I never signed your contract,' retorted Elizabeth.

Mr Darcy's grey eyes widened in surprise, then turned dark and stormy. His brow creased and his mouth twisted. It was clear he was having some internal struggle, fighting against some inner turmoil. All of a sudden, his beautiful

mouth opened and let out a guttural, ear-splitting belch.
'You're not supposed to *do* that!' Elizabeth exclaimed.
'You're a romantic hero!'

Mr Darcy looked abashed. 'My apologies,' he said, 'it must have been the pickled onions I had for lunch.'

Seeing the horrified look on Elizabeth's face, he murmured, 'Look, you were going to discover sooner or later.' He gently traced the line of her jaw with one of his sexy index fingers. 'I fart as well.'

'No, no, no!' cried Elizabeth, covering her ears with her hands. 'Do not puncture my fantasy! You are *not* like other men!'

Mr Darcy looked apologetic. 'Should I resume my glowering?'

'Pray, do that.'

Mr Darcy resumed his glowering.

'What is wrong, Elizabeth?' he rasped. 'I cannot bear to see you unhappy. You must always be honest and open with me, or I shall have to spank the living daylights out of you.'

Elizabeth's jaw set firm. 'You have wounded me deeply, although these past few weeks I did not know it.'

'I do not comprehend you.'

'Can you deny that it was *you* who came between Jane and Mr Bingley? Who condemned her for the inferiority of her connections, and convinced Mr Bingley that a match with someone so decidedly beneath his station in life would be nothing but disadvantageous?'

'There is no denying that I did everything in my power to separate my friend from your sister, and indeed, I rejoice in my success.'

'How so? Jane will never recover from this great disappointment, and as for Mr Bingley, if you think he will be happy with Georgiana, you are mistaken.'

'Georgiana?' Mr Darcy exclaimed. 'What has she to do with it? She will never marry,' he continued. 'She has no interest in matters of the heart.'

'Then why, *why* did you encourage Mr Bingley to quit Netherfield?'

Mr Darcy stood up abruptly, and began to pace about the room. 'I believed, at the time, that my designs were for the benefit of all,' he said stiffly. 'Mr Bingley is a simple soul. You must have noticed he is not the brightest button in the sewing box.'

'And how does this relate to Jane?' asked Elizabeth indignantly.

'I feared she would soon tire of his boundless puppy-like enthusiasm, his general ignorance of world affairs, and especially his catchphrase, "Laters, Baby", which is frankly irritating beyond words.'

Elizabeth nodded. 'A fair point well made, Mr Darcy.'

'It seemed inevitable that she should soon turn from him, and transfer her affections to someone less dim. I wished to save Mr Bingley before he had fallen too deeply in love, and I did so by convincing him that on a Hawaiian surfing holiday packed with hot young Spring Breakers, he might find someone with bigger breasts.'

'But surely that was not your decision to make?'

'I am rarely wrong about these things,' Mr Darcy said ruefully. 'My own first love came to an unhappy end ...'

Elizabeth bristled. 'You refer to Lady Catherine, I suppose?'

Mr Darcy's eyes widened in surprise. 'No ... I am talking about the first recipient of my affections, when I was but a boy.' He sighed. 'Mrs Pickles.'

'The bear that you so cruelly stole from Mr Whackem?' Elizabeth exclaimed. 'You had tender feelings for her? But Mr Whackem said you treated her cruelly, and whipped her daily!'

'Oh, Elizabeth,' Mr Darcy smiled sadly. 'I loved that bear with all my heart! It is true, we indulged in mutually pleasurable spanking sessions, but I would never have hurt her.'

'She was Mr Whackem's bear!'

'Not so, she was mine, given to me by my father. Whackem stole Mrs Pickles from *me*. Whackem, as you know, is charming and erudite, and Mrs Pickles's head was easily turned.'

Elizabeth shook her head, trying to clear her thoughts.

'I confess, I do not know what to think. This is all so confusing. All this stuff about Mrs Pickles wasn't in *either* book.'

'It is an awkward plot device indeed,' Mr Darcy remarked sadly. 'The readers will no doubt find it clunky. But it is my sincere hope that they will retain some sympathy for the author, who is clearly making an effort.'

He reached out and caressed Elizabeth's cheek. 'May I boff you now?' he asked hopefully.

Elizabeth paused. He had driven asunder his own best friend and her dear sister. He had withheld the fact from her, and shown no remorse. He was arrogant, cold and lacking in any finer feelings.

She looked up into his *freakin' hot* face and sighed. 'Oh, go on, then.'

That night, Elizabeth dreamt of giant otters beating each other to death with hunks of cheese. *Holy drug-induced psychosis!* she thought as she shook herself awake. *I must ask Mrs Jones not to put laudanum in my cocoa.*

Sitting up, she wrapped her bedcover more closely

about her naked body. The fire in her bedchamber had long gone out and the room was icy. And then she heard the music – a few lilting notes of a lovely yet melancholy air, echoing mournfully through the darkness.

As if drawn by some mysterious giant magnet, Elizabeth rose from the bed, shivering as her bare feet touched the cold wooden floor. Following the sound, she made her way through the dark corridors and deserted rooms of the house to find its source. At the drawing-room door she paused. Fitzwilliam Darcy was sitting alone on the floor, surrounded by toys. By his side was a hoop and a stick, scuff marks betraying their frequent use; a regiment of lead soldiers lay scattered alongside them. Cross-legged and naked, illuminated only by the light of a single candle, Mr Darcy was turning the handle of a brightly decorated music box, his expression as forlorn and as mournful as the music. In the soft light his beautiful, sculptured face had an otherworldly air, *like a fallen angel,* thought Elizabeth. Round and round the handle turned, while Mr Darcy remained utterly absorbed in the task – round, round and round again. *He plays so beautifully,* thought Elizabeth, mesmerized by the sight of his long fingers, those same fingers that had earlier probed her deepest nooks and crannies.

Just then, the jack-in-the-box popped up with a loud metallic clang. The noise appeared to startle Mr Darcy and he let out a wail of alarm. Hot tears began to course down his beautiful face.

All Elizabeth's compassionate instincts were awakened. Oh, poor Mr Darcy! He may have been a cold and haughty, unbearably arrogant sex pest, but, beneath all of that, he was just a frightened little boy.

'That was a very sad melody.' Elizabeth spoke gently, so as not to startle him. 'How long have you been playing?'

Mr Darcy looked up, his grey eyes still glimmering with tears. 'About half an hour,' he replied softly. 'I could not sleep.'

Instinctively, Elizabeth reached out a hand to touch his bare chest. Mr Darcy flinched and shrank back.

'Ooooh, get off!' he shrieked, flapping his hands wildly.

Elizabeth checked herself at once. Overwhelmed by the vision of his beautiful naked body, she had entirely forgotten Mr Darcy's strict 'no touching' rule.

'Does my touch bring back painful memories from your time at Beaton?' she asked softly.

Mr Darcy appeared nonplussed. 'No, it's just your hands are freezing.'

Slowly, he began to turn the handle of the music box again. Silvery notes tinkled in the air.

'Did your mother play?' Elizabeth enquired. She recalled seeing a portrait hanging above the staircase of a handsome-looking, dark-haired woman seated at a pianoforte.

'I never talk about my mother!' Mr Darcy said savagely, with such force that Elizabeth was shaken.

'Why?' she enquired.

Mr Darcy's jaw twitched, and his eyes grew cold as flint.

'Don't ask me that, Elizabeth,' he growled. 'Anything but that.'

Although he looked menacing – dangerous, even – when angry, Elizabeth knew she must persist. There was so much she wanted to know, so much that would explain why Fitzwilliam Darcy was such a fucked-up SOB.

'She was a beauty therapist,' Elizabeth ventured. 'I know that much.'

Mr Darcy gave a harsh, bitter laugh. 'A beauty therapist! That was not all she was.'

'Why can't you tell me more?'

Abruptly, Mr Darcy stood up, his enormous penis swinging like a pendulum.

'Because I hated her!' he shouted. Elizabeth started. He sounded so vehement, so full of loathing.

'She met my father – the best of men, the kindest, the most honourable – in her salon in London, when he went for a full-body wax,' he snarled. 'Except this was no ordinary salon.'

Elizabeth was silent, watching him. He paced up and down, his eyes fixed upon the floorboards, as if the memories were threatening to overwhelm him.

She prompted gently: 'They offered extras?'

Mr Darcy nodded grimly. 'Indeed. So my mother was … was …'

'A back, sack and crack whore,' Elizabeth murmured.

'That is correct.' Mr Darcy's shoulders shook and for a moment Elizabeth wondered whether he might begin to cry again. Instead, he picked up the jack-in-the-box and held it close to his chest. Elizabeth felt a wave of tenderness overwhelm her.

'But surely …' she said tentatively, 'you cannot know what circumstances led your mother to that fate? You cannot blame her entirely. You, who have worked so tirelessly with fallen women yourself, must have some sympathy for her plight.'

Mr Darcy sighed. 'If only that were all, Elizabeth,' he murmured. 'But you see, my mother never loved me. She was neglectful, cold and distant. When she left the salon to marry my father, she developed other interests.'

Elizabeth's eyes widened.

'She became obsessed with ornithology,' Mr Darcy continued, 'with studying the birds that lived in the lakes and grounds of Pemberley. Nothing else mattered, it was all she talked of. Her specialism was ducks.'

Elizabeth had a terrible feeling she knew where this was going.

'So she was ... a quack bore?'

'She was, for many years, then mammals became her hobby. When she opened her yak store ...'

'Pray, stop now. I have heard enough,' Elizabeth exclaimed.

'Now can you see why I resent her so?' Mr Darcy burst out. 'She was never a true mother to me. If it hadn't been for her best friend, Lady Catherine, taking an interest in me, I would be lost.'

Elizabeth bridled. 'Some would say that Lady Catherine's interest in you was malign. That had she not exerted her influence over you, your character would have been less inclined towards darkness.'

'That is not true.' He smiled lasciviously, and the other Fitzwilliam, the sex-crazed one, was back. 'She made me what I am today. Which means you must get back to bed, Miss Bennet. I want you well rested and ready for more rumpy pumpy tomorrow.'

Rumpy pumpy? That sounded so ... *hot*. Elizabeth felt her secret parts clench in excitement.

'I wondered whether, before the *rumpy pumpy*' – Elizabeth flushed just saying the words – 'we might perhaps take the chaise into the hills and picnic there? I hear there are most excellent views all the way to Yorkshire.'

Mr Darcy gave a sardonic smile. 'I am not the picnicking kind, Miss Bennet. I do not do dainty cakes and pastries and polite conversation. Although I *did* once have a memorable al fresco experience with a veal-and-ham pie ...' Mr Darcy appeared lost in thought for a moment. 'No, Elizabeth, my tastes extend only to darker things.'

'So, you have *never* enjoyed innocent pastimes with a woman, only lewd acts?' Elizabeth asked, aghast. 'Have you never played cribbage, or discussed poetry with a paramour?'

'Never, Miss Bennet.'

'You have never enjoyed a turn about a formal garden, or played croquet or ringtoss on the lawn?'

'No. Well, maybe the last one.'

Elizabeth could find no comfort in his honesty. Although he had, from the outset, made it clear what she could expect from a life of sexual slavery at Pemberley, she inexplicably found herself wishing for more. An orgasm, for instance, would be nice.

Elizabeth had been a good deal disappointed in not receiving any letters from Jane since her arrival at Pemberley, but eventually her repining was over, as two letters arrived at once. One was clearly marked that it had been mis-sent elsewhere, a fact that Elizabeth found unsurprising, given that it was marked, simply, 'Elizabeth @ The Sex Dungeon'.

She opened the mis-sent letter first. It contained news of Longbourn and her family's parties and engagements, but the latter half, evidently written in haste, gave more important intelligence.

'Something has occurred of a most unexpected and serious nature,' Jane wrote. 'What I have to say relates to poor Lydia. A message came at midnight last night, from the barracks, to inform us that she was gone off to the BookExpo in New York with Mr Whackem. It seems, unbeknownst to any of us, that Mr Whackem and Lydia had lately been in discussion about – forgive my indelicacy, Lizzy – *work*, and Lydia's head was quite turned by thoughts of a career; you know how vain and headstrong she is. It seems Mr Whackem has somehow enticed her to join his publishing house, with promises of a salary and future advancement. Lydia left a few lines for us, informing us of their intentions to visit a number of trade fairs in the US. But as yet we know no more. Be assured, Lizzy, I shall write again when we have more news.'

Without allowing herself time for consideration, Elizabeth, on finishing this letter, instantly seized the other. It had been written a day later than the conclusion of the first, and read as follows:

> By this time, dearest sister, you will know of our fears that Lydia now has a *job*. I am afraid I have worse news for you, and it cannot be delayed. We now hear, through associates of Whackem's, that he has little intention of providing Lydia with a salary. She is to be an *unpaid intern*, and receive no remuneration for her pains. It is scandalous! Poor, foolish Lydia. To be enticed with promises of advancement in the publishing world, only to be duped into doing the photocopying, picking up Whackem's dry cleaning and organizing the office Christmas party for *nothing*. Our one consolation is that she is not the first young lady of respectable birth to suffer in this way.
>
> There is not much more to tell. Our stepfather has gone to Bristol, to see if he can catch Whackem and Lydia before they sail. Mother is beside herself with grief and keeps to her room; she says she fears Lydia will never be deflowered now, and will doubtless go to London and become a lesbian. As for myself, I cannot help but think the worst. If Whackem is to use Lydia in this cruel way, she is lost. She will never wish

to return to a life of respectable gentility – of découpage and needlework and staring at the wainscoting – once she has sampled the sinful life of a publishing assistant. She will burn her stays and become a feminist!

'Oh, what to do?' cried Elizabeth, darting from her seat as she finished the letter, and making for the door, as if to pursue the unhappy couple herself. At that moment, Mr Darcy appeared. Elizabeth's wild countenance made him start, but before he could speak, she hastily exclaimed: 'I beg your pardon but I must take my leave. There are events unfolding at Longbourn that require my attention, and my departure cannot be delayed.'

'My God, what is the matter?' Darcy asked urgently, his smoky-grey eyes full of concern. 'Are you ill? Can I get you a bacon sandwich?'

'No, I thank you,' she replied faintly, endeavouring to recover herself. 'I am quite well. I have just received some news from Longbourn which has distressed me, that is all.'

Anxiously, she began biting her nails. Darcy made a low, guttural growling sound.

'Don't do that, Elizabeth,' he murmured. 'You know what it does to me.'

'Forgive me,' said Elizabeth, dropping her hands into her lap. 'I did not mean to set your passions aflame.'

Mr Darcy's eyes were cloudy and intense. Was his conjunctivitis *ever* going to clear up?

'Bend over, Elizabeth.'

'Mr Darcy, this is neither the time nor the place,' entreated Elizabeth.

'I am going to give it to you – hard.'

'Oh, for pity's sake, desist, Mr Darcy, I beg you!' Elizabeth cried. 'I do not wish to receive it at this particular moment in time, hard or otherwise! If you truly want to be of assistance to me, please be so good as to order a carriage to take me to town, that I may catch the next post to Hertfordshire.'

'May I not flog you first?'

'I have not a moment to lose.'

'Then I suppose a handjob is out of the question, too?'

'You are correct, Mr Darcy.'

For a moment Mr Darcy's eyes flashed fire. Then his exquisite features seemed to soften, and he gave a regretful sigh. 'Of course I will help you, Elizabeth. I would do anything for you. But just give me a few moments alone first, in my study.' He walked stiffly towards the door. 'By the way, do you happen to have a pocket handkerchief I could borrow?'

Mr Darcy insisted on accompanying Elizabeth in the carriage as far as Derby, and during the journey she explained to him the circumstances of Lydia and Whackem's business trip.

'I cannot help but feel *I* am to blame,' Elizabeth lamented. 'If I had made known to the world even a little of what you told me about Whackem's character and his abominable treatment of your sister, this would not have happened.'

Mr Darcy's jaw was set in a firm line, and his brow was furrowed. 'Is it absolutely certain?' he asked. 'Could it be, perchance, that Lydia failed the second interview, or has not yet signed the contract?'

'It is quite certain. Whackem intends to employ her as soon as possible.'

At the thought of the humiliation, the misery that

Lydia was bringing upon them all, fresh tears sprang to Elizabeth's eyes. 'May I borrow back my handkerchief?' she enquired of her companion.

Mr Darcy shifted in his seat awkwardly. 'Um, you might not want to do that, Elizabeth.'

Elizabeth stared out of the window in misery. 'I still cannot understand why Lydia was interested in a job in publishing in the first place,' she pondered. 'I mean, she doesn't even know the difference between "discreet" and "discrete".'

Twang! One of Mr Darcy's long index fingers shot out and gently brushed away her tears.

'Elizabeth, I cannot bear to see you distressed. It cuts to the heart of my dark soul,' he whispered. He reached into his waistcoat pocket. 'Here is something to make you smile.' He held out his palm towards her.

'Pray, what are these?' asked Elizabeth, gazing with curiosity upon the mysterious oval objects displayed before her.

'They are *love eggs*,' replied Mr Darcy huskily.

Elizabeth's interest was piqued. 'Are they ornaments, Mr Darcy?' she enquired. 'If so, they are a little ostentatious for my taste.'

Darcy smiled darkly. 'No one will see them, Elizabeth. You wear them *on the inside*.'

Elizabeth gasped. Her Subconscious fainted. And even her Inner Slapper poured herself a stiff measure of gin.

'I want you to kneel on the floor of the carriage now, Elizabeth,' murmured Mr Darcy.

Elizabeth hesitated. Taylor was up above, driving the horses – what if he were to discern something untoward?

'Do as you are bid!' Mr Darcy commanded.

Awkwardly, for it was a narrow carriage, Elizabeth knelt down at Mr Darcy's feet.

'Good girl,' Mr Darcy murmured. 'Now, tell me, Elizabeth, tell me what you want me to do.'

Elizabeth swallowed nervously. 'You may do whatever you want ... Sir.'

She felt her skirts being lifted and then, with one powerful hand, Darcy ripped her bloomers into shreds. Elizabeth's body shook in anticipation.

'Brace yourself, Elizabeth,' Mr Darcy rasped, and suddenly she felt a cold sensation in her most unmentionable bodily part.

'Oh!' she gasped in surprise.

'Does that feel agreeable?' asked Mr Darcy in a low, soft voice.

Elizabeth's breath came in little gasps as she grew accustomed to the sensation. 'I believe so,' she panted.

'You may sit up now, Miss Bennet.'

Trembling, Elizabeth straightened up and rearranged herself on the seat opposite Mr Darcy. What a queer sensation! It was both alarming, and yet intensely pleasurable. As the carriage jolted and shook, she became increasingly giddy and distracted. *Oh my!* Mr Darcy watched her with a salacious smile.

'Taylor!' he called up to his manservant. 'Is the Bakewell road still studded with potholes?'

'I believe it is, Sir.'

'Then go that way, will you?'

When Elizabeth finally alighted on the steps of Longbourn, her joy and relief at seeing Jane waiting for her were considerable. Indeed, her felicity almost banished all thought of the love eggs, until Jane commented on her flushed face and unusual waddling gait.

As the sisters affectionately embraced, Elizabeth asked: 'Is there any more news of Lydia and Whackem?'

'None as yet,' Jane replied. 'Stepfather wrote to say he had arrived in Bristol, but there is no sign of them at the port. But that was his final word.'

'And Mama? How does she fare?'

'She is greatly shaken. She asks after you. Pray, go up and see her in her chamber.'

Mrs Bennet, to whose apartment Elizabeth repaired, received her exactly as expected, with tears, lamentations, and tirades against the treachery of Mr Whackem.

'A *publishing executive*? What manner of occupation is that?' she complained. 'Whackem is a scoundrel, a cad and a scoundrel! I was certain Lydia would be seduced by him, and indeed, she was of the same mind. We even bought condoms for her to carry in her reticule, just in case. And now it seems he had little interest in her body at all! He saw only a foolish middle-class girl ripe for the picking, her head easily turned by talk of foreign-rights contracts, royalties and jacket proofs! To offer her work experience, indeed! My daughter, the working girl! I shall never recover from this, never!'

'Do not give way to alarm, Mother,' Elizabeth cautioned. 'Mr Bennet may yet find them before any real harm can be done. If Lydia can be brought back to Longbourn before she has been shown how to use a photocopier, maybe all will be well.'

'That is more than I could hope for,' lamented Mrs Bennet. 'He must find them, and if Lydia will not come home to a life of mindless, soul-destroying domesticity, then he must at least persuade Whackem to pay her a salary. That, at least, would be a consolation. Oh why could Lydia not have considered escort work. There, at least, is an occupation with prospects!'

Elizabeth reassured her mother, and yet privately, she believed there was little hope. Especially when Lydia's own letter, left at the barracks, was read out to her by Jane.

My dear Mama and sisters,
You will laugh when you know where I am gone, and I cannot help laughing myself at your surprise tomorrow morning, as soon as I am missed. I am going to the BookExpo in New York! And if you cannot guess who with, I shall think you all simpletons, for there is only one officer in the militia who runs an independent publishing company as a sideline. Whackem has promised to introduce me to Coleridge, to Lord Byron and many of our other leading literary figures. I am to be his 'Editorial Secretary' – how grand that sounds! I am not to receive a salary to begin with, but if I work hard, and become a team player, I am assured that 'there will be other opportunities within the company going forward'. Just think of all the shoes and reticules I will be able to buy with my first pay cheque! Goodbye, until we meet again. I hope you will drink a toast to my success!
Lydia xxx

The third and fourth Miss Bennets displayed very different reactions to Lydia's missive. Kitty was pleased that her main rival for the attention of the officers had quit Longbourn for good, and therefore announced herself delighted with Lydia's predicament.

'She will be a hatchet-faced, dried-up old bag when she returns!' she said triumphantly. 'I have heard that working for a living does that to a person.'

Mary, however, was typically condemnatory.

'It can only have a detrimental effect on Lydia's character,' she declared. 'She may have been previously vain and silly, but as a business executive, she will become crass, self-deluding, pompous and clueless. We've all seen *The Apprentice*.' And with that she disappeared back into the music room with an anxious-looking Mr Fiddler, who had declared that her lesson was by no means over, not least until she had performed an arpeggio or two.

Every day at Longbourn now was a day of anxiety; but the most anxious part of each was when the post was expected. The arrival of letters was the first grand object of every morning's impatience. But before they heard again from their stepfather, a letter arrived from a different quarter, from Hunsford and Mr Phil Collins. Jane opened it over breakfast, and together the sisters read:

> *My dear Mr and Mrs Bennet,*
> I feel called upon to condole with you on the grievous affliction you are now suffering under, of which we have recently been informed. The death of your daughter would have been a blessing in comparison to this. You are grievously to be pitied, in which opinion I am joined not only by Mrs Collins, but by our dear Lady Catherine de Burgh, who states that no daughter of hers would be seen dead in an office. She agrees with me that one false step in one daughter will be injurious to the prospects of all the rest, as, Lady Catherine says, who would connect themselves now with such a family? I advise you both to throw off your unworthy child from your affection for ever. The only comfort I can give you now in your time of need is to share my own strategy for dealing with misfortune: when I'm feelin' blue, all I have to do, is take a look at you, then I'm not so

blue. You could try that. Although it depends who you're looking at, I suppose.
Yours, Phil Collins

'Pompous twat,' muttered Elizabeth, most unladylikely. Her relief at being Mr Darcy's kinky-sex slave rather than Mr Collins's wife had never been greater. Elizabeth did wonder, however, why Mr Darcy had not written. Was he angry with her for returning to Longbourn?

It seemed, now, from talk in Meryton, that Whackem had left considerable debts behind in the town, owing some £2 at the paper mill, and only a little less at the printers.

'It's clear his company is operating at a loss,' Jane remarked, as the two sisters walked together through the shrubbery behind the house. 'It cannot have been such a success as he made out.'

'He has misled us in every way,' replied Elizabeth. 'His creditors claim the reason for his current financial situation is that some of his latest publications did not sell as well as expected. *The Whackem Off Guide to Racehorses*, for example, only appealed to a niche market, although some of his agricultural titles were successful. *Fifty Grades of Hay* sold excellently, I am told.'

As they emerged from the shrubbery, they saw Cragg the housekeeper hurriedly coming towards them with a letter in her hand.

'Oh, Miss Jane! Miss Elizabeth!' she called out lower-classly. 'An express has just come, with a missive for you from Mr Bennet!'

Immediately, the two young ladies ran towards her, and caught the letter impatiently from her gnarled hand. 'Read it aloud,' Jane entreated Elizabeth.

'My dear girls, at last I am able to send you some tidings of your sister and Mr Whackem. I have discovered their whereabouts, and upon visiting their lodgings, found them busy at it ...'

'Oh no!' gasped Jane.

'... stapling page proofs together into sales packages. I confronted Whackem as to his intentions towards Lydia, and he confessed he could not afford to pay her a living wage as his company is considerably in arrears. However, he has high hopes for selling *Fifty Grades of Seed*, a companion volume to *Fifty Grades of Hay*. To make this liaison legitimate, I have suggested that I give Lydia her share of the £5,000 I had intended to divide among you five girls after my death; if Lydia invests that amount, she will become a partner and director of Whackem Enterprises. All is agreed and settled, and the papers will be signed this week, whereafter we shall return to Longbourn.'

Elizabeth's brow furrowed. 'Whackem would never allow Lydia on the board of directors for anything less than ten thousand pounds,' she mused. 'He is no fool. He has considerable overheads, and has debts to settle. I cannot believe he has agreed to this.'

Jane's brow furrowed, too. They furrowed at each other intensely. 'What are you thinking, Lizzy?' Jane asked.

'That there is more to this than meets the eye. Someone – some mysterious benefactor, as our stepfather has less than two shillings to rub together – must have settled Whackem's other debts, and no doubt invested a considerable sum in his business venture.'

'But who?'

The two sisters thought hard. 'Do we know any fabulously wealthy gentlemen with vested interests in the wellbeing of our family, or at least one of our number?'

Jane shook her head. It was a mystery indeed.

The rest of the week was spent preparing for the return of the wayward business executives. The news was received badly by Mrs Bennet, who spent another two days in bed weeping and lamenting the fact that her youngest daughter had wilfully made herself so unattractive to men. By Wednesday she had rallied, however, and professed herself strong enough to hear about Lydia's boardroom antics.

Elizabeth, sick of this folly, took refuge in her own room, that she might think with freedom. Poor Lydia's situation must, at best, be bad enough, but that it was no worse, she had reason to be thankful. Who could the mysterious benefactor be?

The day of Lydia's return arrived, and Mrs Bennet and her four elder daughters waited on the front steps of Longbourn for a glimpse of the carriage that would carry her and Whackem thither. On sighting it, Kitty gave a shriek of joy, and even Mrs Bennet managed a wan smile.

Lydia's voice was carried on the air: 'That's all very well, Whackem, but does it have legs? We need to make sure it's robust before we take it to market ...'

Now they could hear Whackem's voice, too. 'I'm confused, Lydia – are we still talking about Daisy, my disabled cow, or the new book project?'

The door of the carriage was thrown open, and Lydia stepped out, beaming, and embraced her family warmly. What a change she had undergone! Gone were the ribbon-bedecked bonnet and sprigged muslin gown she used to favour, and in its place, Lydia wore a mannish suit; the jacket had curiously exaggerated shoulders, while the skirt tapered to fit closely at the knee. Her boots were vanished, too, and replaced by dainty shoes with high, spiked heels, and in her hands, she carried a rectangular leather valise with a small handle.

'Look after my briefcase, Lizzy, there's a dear,' she said airily, thrusting the valise into Elizabeth's outstretched arms. 'And Jane!' she declared. 'Whatever is the matter? You look so wan! Are you still waiting for someone to marry you? I do declare, I am glad to be free of all that nonsense.' She giggled. 'I shan't need to moon after officers again. The only balls I'm interested in now are the ones I intend to break in the boardroom.'

Mrs Bennet looked as if she might faint, and indeed, she reeled slightly as Mr Whackem stepped down from the coach behind Lydia. In appearance he was little altered, but he wore a sheepish look, and when Elizabeth's eyes sought his, he gazed down at the gravel as if it were the most fascinating thing he had ever seen.

Lydia swept into the house ahead of her mother and sisters, prattling all the while about how small and unimpressive Longbourn looked in comparison to the Bristol Premier Inn, which had so impressed her with its amenities – tea- and coffee-making facilities in every room, and even a newfangled trouser press.

Kitty was chided for looking fashionable, and Elizabeth for having an attractive glow about her.

'Why Mary!' Lydia suddenly declared, catching sight of her sister in side profile. 'How fat you have become in my absence.'

Mary glowered at Lydia, but, Elizabeth thought, there was some truth in what Lydia had said. Mary had indeed gained weight these past few weeks, especially about her middle, no doubt thanks to her sedentary pursuits of piano-playing and poring over Latin texts. Elizabeth determined to ask Mary to join her in future on her daily jaunts through the woods.

An awkward luncheon followed, during which Whackem and Lydia discussed their plans for expanding

Whackem Enterprises and the shocking rise in European paper prices, while the rest of the family listened and nodded politely.

'We can't tarry long, I'm afraid,' Whackem declared. 'We have a shareholders' meeting.'

'You are not stopping here, at Longbourn?' Mrs Bennet exclaimed.

'No, this was just a brunch meeting,' Lydia said briskly. 'We need to be in Hertford at two o'clock.'

With that she rose from the table and brushed down her jacket. 'Oh, you will never guess who is to be at the shareholders' meeting, Lizzy. Your Mr Darcy!'

Elizabeth blinked in surprise.

'He has invested twenty thousand pounds,' she said happily. 'A very generous gesture. He has, however, stipulated that we are to invest a proportion of that money in a new series of collectors' editions of his pornography etchings.'

So Mr Darcy was their saviour! It was *he* who had rescued Lydia, condemned as she was to a life of penury and disgrace; at least she only had to deal with the disgrace bit now.

'Will you become a feminist now, Lydia?' Mrs Bennet asked with trepidation. 'I know many young ladies are turning to the ideas of Mary Wollstonecraft, but they are doubtless all of them virgins. You do know that men do not favour women with strong ideas?'

Lydia laughed. 'Oh, sod all that, Mother,' she declared. 'No one ever got ahead in business by being a feminist.'

Mrs Bennet gave a sigh of relief.

'No,' Lydia continued. 'I've got a far better plan than that. I'm going to have a sex change.'

✢

Lydia and Whackem's departure left Mrs Bennet in no better spirits than before. Lydia was obviously set on changing gender, Elizabeth had not heard from Mr Darcy and was at risk of no longer being a sex slave, Jane and Kitty were still boyfriend-less, and Mary, frankly, was porky. It was almost enough to drive her back to her bed.

A most fortuitous turn of events, however, took place the following week, which gave Mrs Bennet reason to hope that all would, ultimately, be well. She and her three eldest daughters were at their darning when Kitty suddenly burst into the room.

'What is it, child?' asked Mrs Bennet, who had dropped her bloomers in shock.

Kitty was panting. 'Mr Bingley! He comes hither!'

'What?' shrieked her mother. 'Mr Elliot Bingley, of Netherfield? Are you sure, girl?'

'I saw him on the road from Meryton. He comes on horseback,' Kitty exclaimed. 'And there is someone else with him, but I cannot be certain who it is.'

Elizabeth's heart gave a start. Could it be Mr Darcy, at last? How she had missed his steel-grey eyes, his muscular thighs, his crispy fries and his mutton pies – he had turned out to be a surprisingly good cook.

The news of Bingley's imminent arrival threw the household into a flurry of activity. Jane was sent upstairs to don her most diaphanous, see-through gown and Cragg was summoned to make her mistress's hair presentable. Kitty and Mary were sent out into the garden, to make themselves scarce. Elizabeth sat intently with her needlework, hardly daring to hope that Mr Bingley's return could signify the resurgence of his ardour for her sister.

Presently the visitors reached the house, and after their horses were tethered, they were shown into the parlour.

Cragg made their introduction: 'Mr Bingley, ma'am,

and ... Princess Leilani.'

Mr Bingley burst in in his customary lolloping fashion, like an eager but dim springer spaniel. From behind him, a beautiful dark-eyed girl of about eighteen peeped shyly from beneath a rose-trimmed bonnet. Her complexion was dusky, her hair black as midnight.

Upon seeing Jane, Mr Bingley's own countenance lit up. 'Why, Miss Bennet!' he cried, 'how well you look. I confess, it has been too long since I have been at Longbourn.'

'Indeed it has,' interjected Elizabeth. 'Some seven months and fourteen days. And did you enjoy your sojourn in the South Seas, Mr Bingley? I trust the waves were gnarly enough for your liking.'

Mr Bingley turned to her and bowed politely. 'They were, Miss Bennet. It was radical. But I confess, I did miss Hertfordshire.' And again, he looked at Jane with bright, hopeful eyes.

Princess Leilani at that moment gave a little cough, and Mr Bingley seemed to remember himself.

'Oh, forgive me. Please allow me to introduce my girlfriend,' he said cheerily. 'I won her in a surfing competition in Waikiki.'

Jane turned instantly pale. Elizabeth looked at her with concern.

'I'm afraid the Princess doesn't speak a word of English,' Mr Bingley continued. 'But I had to bring her back with me to England because she's pregnant.'

Jane swayed noticeably in her chair.

'I fear my sister is a little faint, Sir,' Elizabeth cried.

Mr Bingley sprang forward and caught Jane in his arms. 'Then pray, let me take her out into the garden for some fresh air,' he exclaimed. Lifting her gently, he carried her towards the French windows. The Princess's eyes narrowed.

Jane and Mr Bingley were absent for some half an hour, and during that time, although Princess Leilani was offered pastries, tea and a game of cribbage, she refused all entertainment, and sat silently upon a chair, staring fixedly through the window at the garden.

Presently, two figures appeared from the direction of the orchard, wandering across the grass hand in hand. Mr Bingley was beaming with happiness; Jane was no less radiant in her joy.

Princess Leilani began to mutter something under her breath.

'Happy news!' Mr Bingley burst out as soon as they had re-entered the parlour. 'Jane has agreed to become my wife!'

'This is joyous news indeed!' cried Elizabeth, leaping up to embrace Jane.

'I always knew this would happen!' her mother crowed. 'Did I not say, Lizzy, that if Jane were only to allow Bingley access to "below decks", she would secure him?'

Jane's face was alight with happiness. 'Oh Lizzy,' she breathed. 'I dared not hope! I had quite resolved to forget him, but here he is! If only you could share my felicity, and find someone who means as much to you as my dear Bingley does to me.'

Mr Bingley patted Jane's arm tenderly. 'We are to be married as soon as we can. The reception will be held at Netherfield. We ...'

Suddenly, his gaze met Princess Leilani's. 'Oh, golly. I quite forgot,' he said apologetically.

'Whatever will you do?' enquired Elizabeth, as the princess's lovely face clouded in anger.

'Do not worry on that score,' said a familiar voice from the doorway. Elizabeth gasped. *Mr Darcy!*

He strode into the room, his white linen shirt flapping

in the breeze, his breeches hugging his buttocks like limpets stuck to particularly pert rocks.

'There is a perfectly good workhouse in Hertford,' he declared. 'When the baby is born it can be taken there, and I shall find work for Princess Leilani at Hooters.'

How like Mr Darcy to take command of the situation! It was the perfect solution.

'So it is settled,' beamed Mrs Bennet. 'All has worked out felicitously. Or at least for the white people involved.'

Some time later in the afternoon, Jane and Elizabeth were in the parlour when Mr Darcy burst into the room.

'Oh, forgive me,' he mumbled, blushing to the roots of his copper hair. 'I did not mean to interrupt you at Loo.'

'Please, do not worry, Mr Darcy,' Jane said kindly, placing her cards on the table. 'My! What ails you? You seem most agitated.'

'I confess I am, Miss Bennet,' he replied, his grey eyes blazing. 'I must speak to your sister, if I may, alone. It is a matter of utmost urgency.'

Surprise, then pleasure, registered on Jane's lovely face. Perhaps her dearest wish was about to be fulfilled, and Mr Darcy was going to ask Elizabeth to be his wife?

She stood up at once, and, with a knowing smile, said, 'I will go downstairs, Lizzy, and I will endeavour to keep Mama away.'

'Thank you, Jane,' Elizabeth said quietly, a shy smile spreading across her face. She was certain, this time, that Mr Darcy was on the verge of proposing.

'Elizabeth ...' he began. 'I have to ask for your hand.' Elizabeth's eyes filled with tears of happiness. 'Well, it doesn't have to be your hand, strictly speaking,' Mr Darcy continued. 'It could be your mouth, I suppose.'

'Pray, whatever are you talking about, Mr Darcy?' Elizabeth asked, her mind whirling in confusion.

'I have this blessed erection, Lizzy, and I must do something about it.' His eyes locked on to hers. 'I have to have you,' he growled. 'Now!'

Despite herself, Elizabeth felt a familiar tug in her belly. The effect he had on her was so powerful. Truly he was the master puppeteer, and she was the puppet. He pulled the strings, and she danced. Or rather, gave blow jobs.

'Come ...' he said masterfully, extending his hand. 'To your bedchamber. I have some surprises waiting for you there.'

Elizabeth rose and followed him out of the parlour, and up the staircase, as if mesmerized. Mama might come ... Jane might enter without knocking ... All her inhibitions were cast aside like so many layers of flimsy underwear. All she could think about was Fitzwilliam Darcy's perfect body and losing herself in his embrace.

As they reached her bedroom, Mr Darcy scooped her up in his arms as if she were but a feather. With one blow of his boot, he kicked her bedroom door shut behind him, and threw Elizabeth onto the bed.

'Do you trust me, Elizabeth?' he said in a low voice. His penetrating grey eyes were like two sexy moles, burrowing inexorably towards her heart.

Slowly, sensuously, he unwound his grey silk cravat from about his neck and shook it out with a flick of his sexy wrist.

'I do trust you,' she whispered.

'Then close your eyes.'

Elizabeth felt something soft against her face. Mr Darcy was blindfolding her with the cravat, tying it into a knot behind her head. *Oh my!* It smelt of him – of leather, cologne and Doritos.

She heard his footsteps walking to and fro across the room. More sounds – a clink of glasses, the pop of a cork – then she felt the weight of Mr Darcy's body as he sat astride her. *Holy crap, he weighed a bloody ton.*

'Are you thirsty, Elizabeth?' he asked teasingly.

Elizabeth nodded. Desire had rendered her mouth quite parched, and she yearned for refreshment.

She felt Mr Darcy lean in towards her, and then – *oh my!* – his exquisite lips were upon hers, kissing her, probing her with his mouth. Instinctively, Elizabeth opened her own mouth, and suddenly felt wine trickling over her lips. It was warm and full-bodied, with hints of elderflower and liquorice and a playful, cheeky finish. She swallowed, then licked her lips dry.

'More?' Mr Darcy gargled sensuously.

'Oh yes … please!'

Again Mr Darcy bent down, and again Elizabeth drank deep from his lips. Drops of wine escaped from the side of her mouth, and trickled down onto her neck.

'Now,' Mr Darcy murmured, 'you must eat something, Elizabeth. And I have just the thing.'

Elizabeth felt Mr Darcy shifting his body, moving upwards on the bed, so his knees straddled her shoulders. She could feel the heat of him, smell his distinctive body wash. She tensed. What was coming? Nervously, she opened her mouth and waited.

'Mmmmmmmff!' moaned Elizabeth, as her mouth was suddenly filled with meat.

'Do you like that, Elizabeth?' Mr Darcy murmured. His breathing was coming more quickly now, in jagged bursts. 'It's a faggot. Cragg just made a batch. Tasty, isn't it?'

Elizabeth chewed the savoury, juicy meatball – it truly tasted heavenly – and swallowed. More … She wanted more …

'You're so greedy, Elizabeth. Another mouthful, perhaps?'

More meat, more chewing. Flavours oozed out and overwhelmed her: black pepper, thyme, onions … Her senses were overwhelmed; her head reeled with the carnality of it all.

'Oooh, yeah, baby, that's right,' said Mr Darcy sexily. Or cheesily, depending on your point of view. 'Do you want gravy with that?'

'I do, I do!' Elizabeth moaned. Delicious, savoury sauce dripped into her mouth. She swallowed hungrily, licking her lips clean of every last drop. Mr Darcy gave a moan.

'I love to watch you eat, Elizabeth!'

There was a pause, and Elizabeth felt Mr Darcy climb off her body and off the bed. She lay trembling, panting in anticipation. What was happening? Where was Mr Darcy? Then, out of nowhere, she felt hot liquid splashing all over her belly and thighs.

'I have covered you in gravy, Elizabeth,' Mr Darcy said, breathing heavily now. 'If you move at all, you will get it all over the bedcovers. If that happens, *you* will have to pay the laundry bill.'

Oh my! The salty sauce was hot on Elizabeth's skin. She tensed her muscles, willing herself to stay still.

'Oh Lizzy, what shall I do with you now?' She felt one of Mr Darcy's hands cup her right breast.

'My sweet, sweet girl,' he murmured, cupping her left breast in his other hand. 'You. Are. Mine.' She felt yet another hand between her legs. She gave a gasp. How did he *do* that? Her body, almost as if possessed, began to buck up against him.

'Please …' she begged, squirming.

'What do you want me to do, Elizabeth?' he murmured.

Elizabeth began to quiver.

'I need you, inside me,' she groaned. She felt Mr Darcy sit up, and heard the rip of a foil packet.

'What is that?' she asked curiously.

'Oh, I often rip up a few crisp packets before I have sex,' Mr Darcy said airily. 'It helps get me in the mood.'

Rip! Rip! Rip! Elizabeth quivered in anticipation, lifting her hips off the bed in frustration. Then – *oh no!* – she felt a rivulet of salty liquid begin to crawl, slowly, down over her hip towards the bed.

'You bad girl, Elizabeth! You got gravy on the bedclothes.' The tone of Mr Darcy's voice had immediately changed, and he sounded as if he was struggling to contain some violent emotion. 'You disobeyed me.' Mr Darcy snatched the cravat from her face, and she found herself staring straight into angry eyes the colour of a stormy sea.

'What happens when you are disobedient?'

Elizabeth gulped. 'You … chastise me.'

'That is correct.' His voice was cold, distant, almost as if it were coming from another place. 'You have been a bad, bad girl. You will get ten strokes of my rod.'

He was going to allow her to touch him at last? Elizabeth couldn't believe her luck.

'Not that kind of stroke, dumb-ass,' her Subconscious broke in. 'He's talking about the painful kind.'

Elizabeth was crestfallen. She had been close – so close – to actually getting a seeing-to. Would it ever bloody happen?

'Turn over, Elizabeth,' Mr Darcy commanded. Elizabeth felt something stir deep in her belly. Something that felt like resentment.

'I told you to turn over!' Mr Darcy grabbed Elizabeth's hips and spun her so she was face down upon the bed, her face pressed against the pillow, and her naked behind exposed to his scrutiny. Elizabeth tensed her buttocks. Then, realizing this might make her cellulite more obvious, she relaxed them. Her behind wobbled like a sexy pink blancmange.

'My God, Elizabeth,' Mr Darcy gasped. 'You are so ready for me! Prepare yourself for my rod!'

'One!' Mr Darcy cried, bringing something light – a twig, perhaps? A pencil? – down firmly on Elizabeth's tender flesh. Elizabeth heaved a sigh of exasperation.

'Two!' Mr Darcy exclaimed, and again, the twig/pencil thwacked against her skin with minimal effect. She yawned.

'You're a naughty girl, Elizabeth,' Mr Darcy murmured, rubbing his hand over her buttocks gently. 'And you're mine, all mine.'

'Three!' If he hadn't counted, Elizabeth wouldn't even have noticed the third blow. She lay back and found herself thinking, strangely, of England. What a super place it was to live!

'Four!' Again, the twig/pencil made contact, and again Elizabeth was unmoved. Tears began to prick her eyes. This was not what she had signed up for. She had been expecting earth-shattering, brain-melting, heart-stopping orgasms, not this.

'Fluffy kittens!' she cried, tears beginning to streak down her cheeks. 'Fluffy kittens! Fluffy kittens!'

The effect was instantaneous. 'Elizabeth?' Mr Darcy said anxiously.

Sitting up and pulling the sheet towards her body, Elizabeth dragged herself off the bed and headed for the bathroom. It was only when she reached her bedroom door that she remembered that bathrooms didn't come into existence until the Victorian era, so she headed for the armoire instead, stepping in and shutting herself inside.

Squatting on the cupboard floor, she hugged her knees to her chest and sobbed.

'Please, Lizzy, let me in.' Mr Darcy was leaning against the armoire door, his body pressed against it. She imagined she could feel his breath, still ragged from his exertions, hot upon her neck.

'Are you ever, ever going to actually make love to me, Mr Darcy?'

'That's what you want?' he sounded mystified.

'Yes, that's what I want,' she cried. 'All this "naughty girl" this, and "bad girl" that – I'm beginning to think it's all just an excuse to avoid actual rumpy pumpy.' She paused. 'Are you gay?' *Holy heck,* she couldn't believe she'd just asked that question.

There was silence for a few moments. 'No, Elizabeth, I'm not gay,' Mr Darcy said firmly. 'I'm sorry. I wish I could change. I just have this need. My urge to hit young ladies with various household implements, it's part of me. It's probably all my mother's fault.' He sounded so downcast, so forlorn, that despite herself, Elizabeth felt a pang of sympathy. Fitzwilliam Darcy was lost, lost to the dark side.

'Please ... Please, Elizabeth,' he entreated, 'don't hate me.'

'I don't hate you, Fitzwilliam,' Elizabeth replied softly, opening the door just a crack.

'Ooooh! I can see your crack, Elizabeth!' Mr Darcy gave a childish giggle.

Furiously, Elizabeth pulled the door to. 'And puerile, schoolboy humour – is that part of who you are, too?'

There was silence for a moment. Then Mr Darcy spoke, seriously this time: 'I don't think I can change, Elizabeth. It's almost as if I cannot help myself. Smut comes from deep within me. It's as much a part of me as being British, and male.'

'Then I think it would be best if you left,' Elizabeth called out from the sanctuary of the armoire.

'You cannot mean that!'

Fresh tears spilled down Elizabeth's cheeks. 'I do. We cannot be together. I want what you cannot give me, and I cannot give you what you need.'

She heard Mr Darcy's footsteps pacing to and fro. 'Do not do this, Elizabeth. I will be lost without you.'

'Then go back to Lady Catherine,' Elizabeth said bitterly. 'She will take you under her bingo wings. You may flog each other to death for all I care!'

More footsteps, and the door to her bedroom slammed shut. Fitzwilliam Darcy had gone. The only man Elizabeth had ever desired, the only man she had ever loved, etc, etc. Gone, for about the fourth time. It was all becoming a bit predictable.

One morning, about a week after Mr Darcy's departure, as Elizabeth and the other females of the family were sitting together in the dining room, their attention was suddenly drawn to the window by the sound of a carriage, and they perceived a chaise and four driving up the lawn.

The coat of arms – a pair of naked buttocks surrounded by vicious-looking spikes – was unfamiliar, and they could not guess who their visitor might be. Although when Elizabeth noted that the footmen accompanying the carriage were wearing leather thongs and biker boots, she guessed at once.

'I believe Lady Catherine de Burgh is honouring us with a visit,' she said coolly.

Indeed, a few moments later, Lady Catherine herself swept into the parlour, flanked by four flunkies flagellating each other with floggers.

Mrs Bennet, Kitty and Mary curtseyed low, clearly awed by such alliteration. Elizabeth merely tilted her chin in acknowledgement. But Lady Catherine disdained their welcome. Without saying a word, she made for a chair and attempted to sit down, her leather catsuit creaking. It was only on her third attempt that she finally succeeded.

'You do us great honour with a visit, m'lady,' Mrs Bennet trilled, obviously thrilled to have so high-born a guest sitting in her humble parlour.

'That lady, I suppose, is your mother?' Lady Catherine addressed the question to Elizabeth.

'Yes, Madam, she is,' Elizabeth replied coldly.

'Then pray have her fetch me some talcum powder,' Lady Catherine commanded. 'The journey from Rosings was most uncomfortable and I am chafed all over by this new outfit. The leather has not been broken in yet.'

Mrs Bennet hastened out of the room, calling Kitty and Mary to help her, and Elizabeth and Lady Catherine were left quite alone.

Lady Catherine surveyed the room disdainfully. 'You have a very small house, Miss Bennet,' she remarked. 'Not much room to swing a cat o' nine tails.'

Elizabeth smiled. 'I have no interest in swinging, Madam. I spend most of my time engaged in less perverted pursuits, such as gardening and walking.'

Her visitor gave a sneer. 'Gardening and walking? How ever do you hope to ensnare Mr Darcy with interests such as those?'

'I assure you, I have no interest in ensnaring Mr Darcy,' Elizabeth replied. 'He and I are very different characters, and unsuited to be in each other's company.'

Lady Catherine seemed to relax. 'That is so,' she commented. 'He has a dark, kinky heart, and only someone who shares his predilections can ever truly understand him.'

'It is a great shame that he *is* so kinky,' said Elizabeth, standing up. 'He has been ruined, in my opinion, and will never know how to truly please a woman.'

Lady Catherine attempted to stand. She creaked audibly.

'Help me up, girl!' she snapped. Elizabeth stretched out a reluctant hand, and Lady Catherine, seizing it, hauled herself upright. 'Let us take a walk in your garden,' she suggested.

'In those heels?' Elizabeth said incredulously. 'Are you sure?'

'Don't argue with me, Miss Bennet. I wish to see your box. I have heard that it is most impressive.'

Together they proceeded through the French windows and out onto the gravel path leading to the formal garden. Lady Catherine tottered dangerously on her spike stilettos, and clasped Elizabeth's arm for support.

'You must have guessed, I suppose, why I came here,' she remarked.

'I confess, I cannot imagine why you graced us with your presence,' Elizabeth replied, 'unless you have brought news from Hunsford, of Mr and Mrs Phil Collins.'

Lady Catherine narrowed her eyes. 'Do not trifle with me, Miss Bennet. There is one reason and one only for my visit, and that is to command you to break off all contact with Mr Darcy.'

'And I have already informed you that my acquaintance with Mr Darcy, such as it was, has ceased.'

'We both know that is not true,' Lady Catherine said angrily. 'Why, then, would he come to me at Rosings to tell me he does not wish to continue as my Submissive?'

Elizabeth started as if struck. Mr Darcy wished to hang

up his leather hotpants? She could not imagine such a thing!

'I believe that your arts and allurements may have temporarily made him forget what he owes to me, and to himself.'

'My *arts*?'

'Your talk of holding hands, of kissing, of tender touching ...' Lady Catherine's face was screwed up with distaste. 'Mr Darcy is mine,' she continued. 'My plaything, to do with as I please. It has always been so, and it always will be so.'

Elizabeth pictured Mr Darcy passing round the peanuts at Rosings, his eyes downcast, his demeanour humble, his hotpants riding up his well-formed buttocks ...

'But if Mr Darcy does not wish to continue as your slave, does he have no choice in the matter?'

'He does not know his own mind!' exclaimed Lady Catherine. 'You have quite turned his head, with your big, goofy eyes and your fresh, innocent loveliness. Under your influence, he is even considering getting a puppy. The other day, he suggested that instead of anal probing, we might enjoy a jigsaw together.' Lady Catherine gave Elizabeth a withering look. 'No, I will brook no argument. *You* must be the one to command him to return to me.'

Something stirred in Elizabeth. 'Why, Madam, should I do any such thing?' she asked. 'I see no reason why I should help you in your kinky fuckery. Pray, give me a good reason why I should aid you?'

'Because I say so! And I am a dominatrix! Everyone does what I say!'

'Then you are mistaken, Madam,' she said coldly, raising her chin and pulling her shoulders back. '*I* do not do what you say. *I* am Elizabeth Bennet. I am a heroine to generations of young women, who admire me for my wit, my bravery and my indefatigable spirit. It takes more than a dried-up, domineering old bitch who wears way too much make-up to intimidate *me.*'

Lady Catherine's eyes widened in shock. 'You dare to defy me?' she asked, her voice quavering in anger. 'And by the way, I *don't* wear too much make-up. I only have on a bit of mascara and a touch of nude lipgloss.'

'Oh yeah?' cried Elizabeth. 'Well, I've got something else for your face right here!' And drawing back her hand she gave Lady Catherine an almighty slap; the older woman tottered on her spike stilettos for a moment, her arms windmilling wildly, then fell backwards into a gorse bush. Elizabeth surveyed her coldly; Lady Catherine's blonde hair extensions had snagged on the thorns, and her chicken fillets had slipped down to her navel.

'Now then,' Elizabeth mused, bending down to pick up a solid-looking birch branch that lay on the lawn at her feet, 'get onto all fours, you old hag, while I give you a taste of your own medicine!'

The surprise of the rest of the Bennet family at Lady Catherine's visit was nothing to their shock at seeing her hobble back to her carriage, bent double with a birch twig poking out of an unmentionable part of her anatomy. Elizabeth explained, however, that Lady Catherine had slipped on some damp leaves in the orchard and fallen into a pile of sharp branches, with unfortunate results. Thankfully, no more questions were asked, and Elizabeth was convinced that was the end of the matter. She could not believe that Lady Catherine's influence over Mr Darcy had declined so much that he would seek to renew his acquaintance with the Bennet family after such an insult to his godmother, let alone cast off the trappings of his S&M lifestyle.

Yet the very next morning, Mr Bennet called her into his study.

'Lizzy, I have had a letter that has surprised me greatly,' be began. 'I had no idea, none at all, that I had *two* daughters on the verge of matrimony.'

'Whackem and Lydia are to marry after all?' Elizabeth asked in a shocked voice.

'No, my dear, the letter regards you, and our mutual friend Mr Darcy.' Mr Bennet waved the letter in front of her. 'In this very missive, he has asked me for your hand in marriage.'

Elizabeth blanched. She put her hand out to the bookcase to steady herself.

'Are you feeling faint, Lizzy?' her stepfather asked in a concerned voice.

'It is simply that I am shocked,' she replied. 'I am not sure I want to marry Mr Darcy. My experiences so far ...'

Mr Bennet's brow furrowed. 'He has not treated you kindly?'

'He has, in many regards, used me very ill.'

'Has he ever hit you, child?'

Elizabeth nodded. 'He has.'

'And abused you in other ways?'

'Yes, in countless, filthy ways you cannot even begin to imagine.'

'And is he still as arrogant and proud as he was upon your first meeting?'

'Nothing has changed in that regard.'

'Then of course you must not marry him!' Mr Bennet cried. 'I will not have my favourite stepdaughter shackled to such a beast. Oh, wait a minute ...' He glanced down at the letter. 'I forgot, there was a PS somewhere. Let's see ...

Oh, yes, that's it. He says he really, really likes fishing.'
'And?' Elizabeth asked, nonplussed.
'I really like fishing, too!' exclaimed her stepfather.
'The matter is settled then. I shall write at once, giving my permission for Mr Darcy to come to Longbourn and claim you as his bride. Run along now and fetch me a cold beer, there's a good girl.'

Thus it was that Mr Darcy arrived at Longbourn some three days later, accompanied by Mr Bingley. Bingley, who wanted to be alone with Jane, proposed a walk about the grounds, a plan that Mr Darcy happily agreed to, and Elizabeth less happily so. Mr Darcy, she fancied, seemed a little more humble than usual. His arrogant swagger was still in evidence, and his permanent smirk, but his eyes betrayed some inner anxiety. As soon as he was able, he led Elizabeth down a different route from that taken by the newly engaged couple, and together they walked arm in arm through the shrubbery.

'My dear Miss Bennet,' Mr Darcy began, with a formality to which she was unaccustomed. 'I understand you lately received a visit from Lady Catherine de Burgh.'

Elizabeth's countenance betrayed nothing. 'That is correct, Mr Darcy,' she replied, with equal politeness. 'She did us the honour of calling upon us.'

'And I understand that you thrashed her black and blue.'
'I did, Mr Darcy.'

They walked on together for a few moments in companionable silence.

'Am I to understand from this,' Mr Darcy asked in a low voice, 'that I might have cause to hope?'

'To hope for what?' Elizabeth asked, her blue eyes

widening in surprise. 'That I will resubmit to your will, and become your sex slave once again? That I will agree to live an orgasm-free existence at Pemberley?'

Mr Darcy stepped back as if stung. 'You have never climaxed during our encounters?'

Elizabeth flushed, despite herself. 'I do not wish to wound your pride, Mr Darcy, but no, never.'

'How can that be so?' Mr Darcy asked, incredulously. 'Lady Catherine taught me everything there is to know.'

'Then I believe she taught you very ill.'

Mr Darcy's eyes flashed in anger. 'Lady Catherine is well versed in the ways of the flesh!' he exclaimed. 'She was an excellent tutor.'

'She may know about flesh,' cried Elizabeth passionately, 'but she knows little of love, of eroticism, of intimacy. Of truly pleasing a woman!'

Mr Darcy, clearly shocked, quickened his pace. His face was dark, glowering. 'You do not like my Broom Cupboard?' he asked. 'I had thought you were enticed by my dangerous, dark desires.'

Elizabeth shrugged. 'Not really. I mean, yes, it's something a bit different and all that, but have you never thought to leave aside your floggers and your nipple clamps, and just have normal sex once in a while?'

By now Elizabeth was blushing furiously, both from embarrassment and passion, but she was determined to confront Mr Darcy with the truth.

'No, I never have. That's not what I'm about.' Mr Darcy smiled ruefully. 'I've told you, vanilla is not my flavour, Elizabeth.'

Elizabeth gazed into his fathomless grey eyes. What was going on in there? He was so complex, so deep. 'What *is* your flavour, Mr Darcy?'

'Kinky, with lashings of whipped cream and a butt plug

on top.'

Damn Lady Catherine! Elizabeth thought, furiously. And damn Beaton for turning a vulnerable, defenceless young boy into a raging pervert!

Tentatively, Elizabeth reached out a hand and touched Mr Darcy's thigh, as delicately as a butterfly landing on a side of ham. He flinched.

'Please – for me,' Elizabeth pleaded. 'I would like us to try.'

So many emotions flashed across Mr Darcy's chiselled features, like clouds scudding across the sun: uncertainty, fear, anguish ...

'Dammit, Elizabeth,' he said huskily, running his hands through his tousled locks. 'I do not even know whether I'm capable of such a thing. I have been pervy for so long, I fear I am beyond redemption.'

'I do not believe that is true,' murmured Elizabeth. 'Somewhere inside you is a predictable, run-of-the-mill, unadventurous lover. I shall help you. I want to discover the delights of unexciting, Saturday-nights-only, always-in-the-missionary-position sex with you. Come ...' She held out her hand. 'Take a turn about the rose garden with me.'

Mr Darcy's eyes registered shock, and something else, something deeper – fear?

'A turn about the garden?'

'Yes, Fitzwilliam. Can it be so very bad?'

'I have never, *never* simply walked about the garden for enjoyment alone.' Panic was seizing him now. 'Will I be expected to ... to comment upon the flowers, or the view?'

'You will. But you can do this.'

Mr Darcy pulled her close, tugging her hair so her face was turned up to his. 'You are an incredible woman, Miss Bennet,' he breathed. 'You have such confidence in me.

You are doing all this for my sake?'

'I would do anything for you,' Elizabeth replied, tears beginning to pool above her lashes. 'Except fisting, remember?'

Together they began to perambulate the gravel path leading to the orchard, and thence through an arbour into the rose garden. Mr Darcy's body was tense; he moved stiffly, as though preparing himself to flee at any given moment.

'Do you notice the Floribunda roses there?'

Mr Darcy's eyes flashed with panic. 'They ... they are quite lovely, Miss Bennet,' he blurted. 'Very ... yellow.'

Elizabeth patted his hand reassuringly. 'Indeed, they are very yellow. And quite gloriously scented. Would you care to smell one?'

Gently, so as not to alarm him, she plucked a single rose from the bush and held it towards Mr Darcy's face. 'Try it.'

For one moment she fancied Mr Darcy would turn on his heel and run away. He appeared to be wrestling with some inner demons. But at length he seemed to steel himself. His breathing slowed and he bent to inhale the rose's heady perfume.

'Exquisite,' he announced.

Elizabeth beamed with joy. 'Oh, Fitzwilliam,' she breathed. 'You have just experienced a non-sexual pleasure! And you didn't even say, "Watch out for pricks!" or make jokes about bushes as I was sure you would!'

A slow smile spread across Mr Darcy's face. 'Truthfully, those puns did not occur to me,' he said delightedly. 'You have a powerful effect upon me, Miss Bennet.' He bent his lips to hers for a chaste kiss. Elizabeth felt her nether regions stir.

Together they moved towards the love seat at the far corner of the rose garden and sat down. Elizabeth gazed at Mr Darcy's muscular body with longing. 'May I touch you?' she whispered.

Mr Darcy frowned. 'Whereabouts?'

'I thought I might start with your chest.'

Mr Darcy's eye gave a nervous twitch. 'Very well, Elizabeth,' he said, his mouth set firm and his jaw tense. He took a deep breath. 'I am ready.'

'Skip the bloody chest, go straight to third base!' Elizabeth's Inner Slapper hissed. 'You might not get another chance!'

But Elizabeth paid no heed. Slowly, oh so slowly, she slipped one hand inside Mr Darcy's shirt and ran it over his magnificent nipples, gently tracing the lines of his sculpted abdomen. *Jeez, he was ripped!*

Every muscle of Mr Darcy's body was tensed; his eyes were squeezed shut, his breath coming in rasps.

'You must tell me if this is painful for you,' Elizabeth said anxiously. 'You only need say the safe word and I shall stop at once.'

Elizabeth's roaming hands moved down, down towards the buttons of Mr Darcy's breeches. 'My God, Elizabeth,' he gasped. 'Are you sure about this?'

One by one, the buttons popped open, released by Elizabeth's eager fingers. Mr Darcy's breathing was ragged now; his jaw was clenched and the veins in his neck were standing out like guy ropes.

'I think you may need to stop now, Elizabeth,' he gasped, 'as I feel the end is drawing near.'

'Oh!' Elizabeth withdrew her hand. 'So soon?'

'I have told you, it does not take much to bring me to the brink,' Mr Darcy said fervently. 'A table leg is enough to inflame my desires. A quivering jelly upon a plate. Even a word can be enough – I have never been able to visit the Pump Room in Bath for fear of what might occur.'

Elizabeth pondered for a moment. 'Then let us try something,' she said at last. 'Let us make conversation about less ... *stimulating* matters. This will take your mind off the task in hand.'

'How so?'

Elizabeth's hand once again wandered to Mr Darcy's breeches. 'I recall you mentioned purchasing new wallpaper for the library,' she said airily. 'Do you still favour Chinoiserie?'

Mr Darcy gave a groan. 'Chinoiserie ... is so ... last year.'

Elizabeth's hand worked silently, caressing, teasing, tantalizing. 'Might you consider, say, a flocked damask?' Elizabeth continued. 'They are all the rage in Town.'

'Possibly,' Mr Darcy gasped. 'Although a ... *trompe l'oeil* frieze would ... work well. Would you ... not agree?'

Oh my! She was giving pleasure to Mr Darcy! At last! Slipping off the bench, Elizabeth lifted up her gown and then sat astride him, lowering her body down onto his. Oh, the delicious feeling as he filled her!

'The Prime Minister, I hear, has a plaid design in *his* library, printed on satin paper ...'

Mr Darcy's eyes were half-closed, his face tense. Gently, slowly, Elizabeth rocked up and down.

' ... although I hear tell that it is a little garish. Perhaps a *toile de jouy* would be best? A little *démodé*, perhaps, but a classic nonetheless.' Elizabeth's own breathing was becoming uneven now. Her secret parts felt deliciously warm, as if someone had poured honey over her insides.

'*Toile* is worth ... consideration.'

Elizabeth increased her pace. Mr Darcy's hands grasped her hips, and together, they moved as one.

'You could ... simply paint ...' Elizabeth panted.

'Wallpaper would be best,' Mr Darcy murmured.

The bench was shaking now, as the intensity of their lovemaking increased. Elizabeth flung her head back. Her body shook as she felt an intensity building, threatening to shatter at any moment. Mr Darcy cried, 'I am coming ... round to the idea of ...' He gave a loud gasp, and his muscles tensed, 'FLOCK!' he shouted, as his body found its release. Elizabeth's insides dissolved into nothingness as waves of pleasure washed over her, and she collapsed against him, breathing heavily, her fingers entwined in his hair.

'Oh, Fitzwilliam!' Elizabeth cried, stroking his copper mane. 'You have done it! You have experienced run-of-the-mill lovemaking!'

Mr Darcy sighed and held her close. She breathed in his musky, Doritos-y scent.

'My Lizzy,' he murmured. 'You. Are. So. Special. You have done so much for me. You have entered my Blue Broom Cupboard of Seriously Kinky Shit. You have let me whack you with vegetables, and pummel you with newspapers. If ordinary sex is what you want, you shall have it.'

'Let us meet halfway, Fitzwilliam,' she murmured, her face still buried in his hair. 'I shall sign your contract. How about Monday to Friday we have vanilla sex, then at the weekends we let our hair down and do all the kinky stuff?'

'Oh, Lizzy!' Mr Darcy cried, squeezing her so tightly she felt she might faint. 'You've made me the happiest pervert alive!'

Not everyone was delighted by Elizabeth and Mr Darcy's happy news. Kitty was downhearted to be the only daughter now left at home; Lydia having finally sailed for New York on business, Jane being ensconced at Netherfield, and Mary having been despatched to the country to give birth to Mr Fiddler's baby.

'Mary is not supposed to have got a shag at all!' Kitty raged. 'She's clearly the least attractive, and in the original book she is destined to remain a virgin all her life!'

'But this is the sexed-up version,' her mother pointed out. 'Classics with bonking are all the rage now. Think of *Northwanger Abbey*, or *Mansfield Pork* …'

'Or *Enema*,' pointed out Elizabeth. 'I do believe Miss Austen intended *that* particular novel to be about an interfering matchmaker, not one Mr Tightly's penchant for anal sex.'

Elizabeth's new home was, of course, to be Pemberley, and although she missed her family greatly, she soon came to love it, and its inhabitants, even more than Longbourn. She and Mr Darcy kept to their agreement, with Saturday nights and Sundays, after church, reserved for kinkery fuckery, and the rest of the week devoted to unremarkable, nothing-to-write-home-about rumpy pumpy. In fact, all was felicity and concord, and that would have been an appropriate ending, had not one thing intruded upon their happiness.

'What, pray, do you keep in the shed at the bottom of the garden?' Elizabeth asked one morning, on returning from her daily perambulation about the grounds.

Mr Darcy's face darkened. His eyes turned from steel grey to black iron. 'That I can never tell you, Elizabeth,' he murmured. 'Never. It is my darkest, darkest secret.'

Elizabeth swallowed nervously. 'I thought I knew all your dark secrets.'

'Not this one.' Mr Darcy's body was tense, as if he was expecting a blow to fall. 'If you knew what was in my shed, you would know how corrupted my soul is, how I can never be saved.'

Oh, Mr Darcy! All Elizabeth's compassionate instincts were roused. She stretched out a hand to touch his face, but he instantly recoiled.

'You have seen my Blue Broom Cupboard of Seriously Kinky Shit,' he said in a strangled voice. 'But you do not know what lies within my Sage-Green Shed of Shocking Artefacts.'

Elizabeth gasped. There was more? More licentiousness? More perversion? She certainly hoped so.

'Please,' she entreated. 'I've told you before, I want to know the real Fitzwilliam Darcy. There is nothing you can show me that can shock me.'

'You will never love me again. Never.'

'Try me.'

'Very well.' Mr Darcy looked on the verge of tears. 'Then come ...'

The Sage-Green Shed lay at the far end of the wildflower garden; covered in ivy and overgrown with lichen, it blended beautifully into its surroundings, and looked to be no more than an attractive addition to the landscape. A winding path led to it, and Mr Darcy strode ahead, his gaze fixed, not saying a word. Elizabeth felt her chest palpitating with anxiety. Could she cope with what was inside? What perversions lay within?

'Behold!' Mr Darcy announced, throwing open the door. 'My fifty shades ...'

Holy shit! Lampshades of every kind, of every aspect and design leapt out at Elizabeth. Shades trimmed with tassels and ribbon, elaborate candle sconces, storm lanterns, coloured glass shades for newfangled gas lamps ... Many of the lamps had been illuminated, and the candlelight made them dance menacingly, demonically.

'My collection,' Mr Darcy breathed. 'Aren't they exquisite?'

Elizabeth had not prepared herself for this. She struggled for breath. It was too much, too, too much.

'This one,' purred Mr Darcy, picking up a miniature chandelier, 'I bought for a few farthings at a French flea market. Beautiful, isn't she?' The tinkling of the chandelier's crystal droplets sounded, to Elizabeth's ear, just like cackling laughter, mocking her. Mr Darcy ran his hands sensuously over the rim of a storm lantern. 'My shades are my life, Lizzy. If we are ever to make a life together at Pemberley, you must accept my obsession. I am always looking out for more trimmings, for the perfect polish for brass fittings, for replacement tassels. I come out here most evenings simply to stare at my shades.'

He collected bloody lampshades? Elizabeth felt her legs starting to give way beneath her.

'Elizabeth?' Mr Darcy asked, his voice full of concern.

Her senses reeling, Elizabeth was already stepping backwards out of the shed. She was aware that she was speaking, but found it hard to recognize her voice as her own.'

'This, Sir, is the lamest plot line I have *ever* encountered in a novel!' she cried. 'It beggars belief. I'm not even sure lampshades *per se* are in use in 1814, given that gas lighting will not become widely adopted until later in the century.'

Mr Darcy stepped back in shock. 'You find it lame? It is a fairly cheap gag, granted, but surely it has some small value?'

Elizabeth shook her head. She could not believe her dreams were being shattered so. The non-orgasmic sex she could take, the arrogance that had led Mr Darcy to sunder her sister and Bingley, but *this*? This turned the whole title of the book upside down, and made a mockery of the entire premise. This she could not forgive.

Turning, she began to run, despite her light-headedness

and shock, back across the wildflower garden to the safety of the house.

'Elizabeth! Wait!' cried Mr Darcy.

She ran on, tears blinding her, until Mr Darcy grabbed her by the shrubbery.

'Where are you going, Lizzy?' he asked desperately. 'Please don't run away. Try ... try to understand.'

Elizabeth shook her head wildly. She could not look into those intense grey eyes, for fear they would melt her resolve. 'No ... no ... I must return to Longbourn. Let me go at once, I beg you.'

Mr Darcy released her shrubbery and straightened up, and when he spoke his voice was cool and distant.

'I feared my first instincts were correct, Miss Bennet. You cannot handle my fifty shades. Not many women can.'

Curiosity pricked her. 'Did you show your other Submissives?'

His mouth tightened. 'I did. And most fled. I had hoped you would be different.'

By now the tears were coursing down Elizabeth's cheeks. 'You have misled me, Sir. You encouraged me to believe that "fifty shades" referred to your complex, multilayered personality. Not ... not *this*.'

Fifty *lampshades*? It was just a bad joke.

'Wait, let us discuss this rationally,' Mr Darcy said calmly. 'We have two choices as far as I can see. We can leave this hanging, and there could be a sequel ...'

They both paused, considering the implications. It would mean even more double entendres, more schoolboy-level sexual innuendo, with the puns becoming progressively weaker and weaker as the author ran out of rude words – it would be, frankly, exhausting.

'Could you honestly be bothered to go through it all again?' Mr Darcy asked. Elizabeth wiped the tears from her cheeks with the back of her hand.

'Not really,' she confessed. 'I think it's probably best to make this book a one-off.'

'In that case, should I just shut the shed door?' Mr Darcy asked. 'We can just pretend this never happened.' He looked so hopeful, so vulnerable, that Elizabeth could not find it in her heart to deny him.

'Very well,' she breathed. 'Let us shut the door, Fitzwilliam.'

'You know what they say – when one door shuts, another one opens,' Mr Darcy said salaciously, with a wicked glint in his eye. 'How about we open your back door, Elizabeth?'

'Let us save that for another time, Mr Darcy,' Elizabeth said curtly. 'I believe it would be best to end this book on a traditional note.'

'You mean, "they lived happily ever after"?'

'That would be perfect.'

Mr Darcy sighed. 'Very well, Elizabeth, if it pleases you. We will live happily ever after.'

Elizabeth gazed deep into his mesmerizing, steel-grey eyes. He was a complex, fucked-up, psychologically unstable billionaire, but he was *her* billionaire, for ever and ever.

'The end,' she breathed.

Also available from Michael O'Mara Books

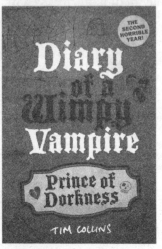